SCHOOLBOY

SCHOOLBOY

MARTIN KEAVENEY

PENNILESS PRESS PUBLICATIONS

www.pennilesspress.co.uk/books

Published by

Penniless Press Publications 2023

ISBN 978-1-913144-52-4

Cover: Paul Butler

To Brendan

I

I am dying to start. I stand halfway up the hill, across from the post office, at the end of the drive to our house. I grind the soft black shoes mam got me last week on the gravel. My sister is looking out through the sitting window, sticking her head between the curtains.

I am apprehensive, but excited. I just can't wait. I am holding my new 'Jack's Army' schoolbag, full with copies and text books. My hair is tied back in a ponytail, I can feel the curls at the end bouncing gently against the nape of my neck.

I just want to get started! I feel clean and warm. It's a lovely morning. It's cloudy, but mild. It's green. The village I come from is noted for its greenness. It's a yellow bus I will be getting. I have seen Agnes, the girl across the road, get this bus for years. She used to babysit me. But she is finished school now.

If I could just get the first day over, that would be great!

For nights, I have been dreaming of the first day, imagining myself getting up, putting on the neatly creased grey trousers, the light blue shirt, the navy jumper with the school crest. I feel taller and more complete in them.

My sister is at the front door.

'Go in, will ya!' I say. I don't want that kind of embarrassment, on the first day, the baby sister waving me off. I told mam and dad not to come out. Mam was even a bit teary this morning, but she stayed inside. They even wanted to take a picture of me.

'Mam says are you going wearing the hat?'

'I am yeah…'

I take the black beret out of the schoolbag. I wasn't sure, but why not? Express yourself. That's my philosophy. I had a look at a few philosophy books over the summer. Mam went to college as a mature student. She said I should skip secondary school and go straight to University. I don't know if she was serious. The books were kind of tricky to understand. It looks complicated, but I could do it, if I tried hard enough. I wouldn't mind skipping school and going straight to the big lecture halls. I went along with mam a few times. I fit on the beret, pressing it down to the left side.

Teeth smell nice and clean. I brushed them this morning. I usually just brush at night, but I said I would today as well.

If I had the first day over, I could relax. I'd know what to do, then. I'd know where everything is. In the village school down the road, I left being amongst the biggest, in sixth class. My brother had just started in baby infants. For years, I've wished he was nearer my age so I could play with him. I try football but he's only five. My sister is ten but she just wants to play house. Sometimes I get her to play in goal and I play in the garden with imaginary team mates.

Some people go into secondary school with someone ahead of them, like Quirke. Quirke's brother is going into Second Year now. Quirke says it's good to have someone you know ahead of you, who'll look after you.

I hope it won't matter. I heard a few horror stories about this school. Flushing heads down toilets and things. My brother won't be much use to me.

Quirke is always exaggerating though. It's probably nonsense. It's like Doyle on about horror films that change your life forever and when you watch them they're just silly. He's the youngest in his family, but he has a rake of sisters, I think it's six. They're all older than him. He's coming over this evening for a few shots of the football or a game of *Sonic The Hedgehog* if it's raining. We'll talk about how today goes.

If I could just get the first day over with!

Doyle had to stay back this year. He's clever enough, but he doesn't ever do anything at school only cause trouble. He does the stupidest things, like blocking the sink in the toilet with toilet paper and running the water, flooding the school corridor. Pure nonsense stuff.

I did fairly well in sixth class. I don't mind maths and English. Irish is a bit of a challenge. I did aright in the summer tests The Master set us. Ninety percent in English, eighty-five in maths. I did not bad in Irish, even though it was a bit hit-and-miss. History and geography, they're easy, you just learn off dates and places. I was top of the class.

'You have brains to burn,' The Master said. Funny expression. Imagine burning your brains. But Doyle failed most of the tests. His mother must have went bananas. He had to repeat. It's very annoying. I suppose there's Melvin. Melvin's actually a year older than me but he failed a few things in infants or something and he somehow ended up in my class. But he's strong, Melvin is.

Still, I'm looking forward to it. Five years, and then I'll be off to Uni. I'm going to be a journalist. I love making newspapers and magazines. I wouldn't mind working in a TV station. But I love writing up the news. Every morning all summer I was making a four-page newspaper, in the centre of copies. I gathered local reports from the radio, had a section on household items, farm jobs, like me, dad and granda in the bog, stuff like that. I wrote an editorial, some world news and had a sports page on the back. Liverpool just missed out on the double last May. They're favourites for the title again this year.

I like writing stories too, but that's a waste of time, dad says.

Oh, here she comes. A surge of something in my stomach, like when it's Christmas Eve and you're waiting for Santy. I still like Christmas. The bus is yellow and fairly dirty. So that's 'Mad-dog'. That's what they call the bus-driver, Quirke said. He does look fairly cross. I wave a hand to my sister. Mam and dad are at the sitting room window. See ya! Mam's wiping her eyes with a tissue. I try to put on what I imagine to be a consoling expression. Mothers!

The door splits into two panels and opens. There are two steep steps. I clamber up, pulling the handle to haul myself onto the floor of the bus. The panels slam and the bus jolts as Mad-dog lets up the clutch.

'Your ticket, ing,' Mad-dog says, as we move off.

The bus jerks as it turns the corner at the top of the hill. I almost fall. Mad-dog grabs the ticket, looking just at the date. He stares at me. My cap must not be straight, he squints a little.

'All right, ing,' he says, handing the ticket back. The engine roars, and I jolt across the aisle, banging my forehead against an iron bar in front of the first seat. My beret has slid over my eyes and I can't see anything. The schoolbag swings and I grapple for the iron bar to stabilise myself. Anchored finally, I pull up the beret.

There's Melvin, a few seats down the aisle. He sits at the window, a spare seat next to him. Handy!

'How's craic,' I say, as I sit down. He doesn't say much. He seems nervous, does Melvin. I don't know why. It's just a new school. I can't wait. I don't look around much, though. Everyone is a lot bigger than me.

There is a loud scraping noise across the top. I look back. Low lying branches. Nobody takes any notice. Mad-dog fairly drives this thing, zooming around corners. You can feel every bump on the road. I can see how he got his name now.

There is a smell of tobacco. Cigarettes actually. Not pipe smoke like with Granda. I love the smell of the chestnut pipe. But it's a stupid habit, dad says, deliberately putting your health at risk. He was smoking when he was seven. It wasn't thought to be bad for you then. He gave up years ago. Dad says a couple of pints of stout is no harm, when you are old enough. He had his first pint at eighteen. I probably won't drink until I go to college either.

I look down the bus again. A line of silhouettes mark out the back window.

'What are you looking at?' a voice says, and I look back toward Mad-dog. I have a funny feeling, like a hand grabbed the pit of my stomach.

There are a lot of pick-ups. The First Years have new schoolbags, new jackets, new uniforms, shiny black shoes. The older students' bags are worn around the edges, there is something tired about them. Everyone seems to know everyone.

Farrell, taller now than when I last saw him in May, Quirke, still just over four foot six, I suppose, and the mid-sized shape of O'Brien get on. They all live beside each other. Farrell sits beside Quirke half way down the bus and they strike up a conversation that sounds like it continues on from the weekend.

After the bus seems to have collected all, Mad-dog really opens her up. The engine wails up and careers down every hill. The bus is cold, an icy draft comes from underneath. Melvin is even quieter than usual, he must be awful nervous altogether.

We come into the one street town. Beside the school entrance is an abandoned hotel. I look closely at the boarded up windows, the decrepit sign, the obsolete lunch menu board.

Branches brush the side of the bus as it drives up the avenue. Mad-dog doesn't bother slowing at the speed ramps and we all bounce off the seats. We pull in at a small car park, near the school entrance. It's a small square porch type thing, with a few panels of glass. Not much of an entrance really.

I was here at the enrolment night back in March. It was dark then though, and it all seemed years away. Now it's morning, and it's bright and I am wearing the uniform, the uniform I'd seen Agnes across the road wearing for years. I even feel a bit scared.

A ginger bearded man in a beige suit stands at the entrance with an important looking blue folder. He waves everyone into the porch and toward a doorway to the right.

'That's Mac,' Quirke says, as we walk in. The Vice Principal. Mac looks bored, his motions robotic, his eyes just dead brown spots in a bland face. The queue in is slow.

'Hey, hey, this way,' Mac is saying.

I hear a shout from behind and look around. A thin tall boy and a smaller large-headed boy casually walk up the avenue. They get to the front of the building and walk toward the side, in the opposite direction to Mac's ushering arm.

'You lads. This way!' Mac says.

They look over, as though surprised. There is something comical about their expression, and I laugh.

They seem to hear me and look toward us. I turn back and follow Farrell down the porch area to the door everyone is walking through. We arrive in a large assembly hall.

More suited men and women are pointing us into areas. There are also tall uniformed pupils with small triangular badges.

It seems the queues are organised to year. We, being the smallest, are ushered to one side, and each year is lining up now across the hall. I see through the tall windows another bus has arrived outside, students fill the hall quickly.

Mac is now standing up on a huge stage, which I have just noticed at one end.

'Hey Brush,' Farrell taps me on the elbow. 'Are you going to take off the hat?'

I realise I should have taken the beret off but I won't remove it now, not having nowbeing told by Farrell.

'Howya,' I say. 'No. I think I'll leave it on.'

'You're some man. What do you think, Melv?' he says to Melvin.

'Alright,' Melvin says.

'See them bucks,' Farrell says, nodding toward the door we came in. The tall and thin boy and his large-headed companion now stand in the door way, looking into the hall. I notice Mac watching them.

'Hey, hey, you two. Get down there,' Mac says.

'Oh, yeah. Idiots, they were going the wrong way. Yer man gave out to them. Are they First Years?' I say.

'I don't know and I don't want to know,' Quirke says, scratching his chin. 'One of them is a son of Jake Marley, you know the fellow that stole all the money.'

I don't know Marley, but I nod anyway.

'And the guy with the massive head, people reckon his father is a complete psycho. Lives in a shed out the road. O'Toole is his name. The brother was telling me to steer clear,' Quirke says.

'They're no idiots, Brush,' Farrell says. I feel like I had laughed at a joke that wasn't funny.

'Hey young lad! Take off that hat!' I look around at a blue chest with the triangular badge up close. It reads 'Prefect'. Above me is a thin-faced student. 'You can't wear that inside.'

I take the cap off, Farrell smirking as the prefect gestures him down the line. My ponytail dances around.

'And what's this?' the prefect continues. Touching, yes, touching my hair.

'You'll not get away with that buck,' the prefect says. 'Mrs Sharpe will talk to you about it.' He walks off. Mrs Sharpe will talk to me about what, I wonder? Style issues?

The lines smooth out. Ahead, I can see some boys from the next village, whom we have played rounders against. Mann, bottle-shaped, stands next to the shorter Corless whose eyes appear to be closed. Behind them is Houston under a thick head of greyish hair. While Corless and Houston are static to the point of appearing unconscious, Mann moves from left to right as though listening to music.

A hush falls over the hall. From a wing of the stage, The Principal emerges. Peter F. Shylock. He is not particularly tall, smaller than Mac but not what you would call short either. He has a long purple skinned face and is bald on top with black patches of hair over his ears. His suit is navy and neat. His eyes are lively but his eyebrows give him a piercing stare.

He walks to the centre of the stage where a microphone is set up. He taps it, making a loud thud come from somewhere and the hall is silent.

'Good morning.' Peter F. Shylock may not be big, but his voice booms.

'I welcome you to the new school year. It is my privilege to have been Principal here since the Department of Education took over this building and grounds from the St. Clare order some years ago. It was one of the wishes of the final Mother Superior, Sister Celia, that this school would promote modern educational methods, discipline and the social development of youths. The Board of Management have indicated they believe we have succeeded and we are determined to continue this proud tradition.

I welcome our returning pupils and the First Years. We look forward to a year of education, enthusiasm and good conduct. I wish to remind all pupils that there are a number of rules and regulations in operation here. Firstly, teachers and other staff are to be respected and obeyed at all times. Secondly, smoking is completely prohibited in the school building, on the grounds, and coming to and from the school either by foot, car or Bus Eireann services. The bus driver is responsible for the welfare of children on the bus and should be considered as authoritive as any of our teachers. Other rules and regulations can be perused by all pupils in the homework diary supplied. First Years should hereafter assemble to be divided into rooms. As usual I conclude Assembly with the Lord's Prayer as Ghaeilge.'

After we all pretend to say the 'Our Father', all of the other lines move out of the assembly hall. We are then queued up to a long table near the stage where we each receive a round green badge, which has our names on it.

'Wasn't too bad,' I say to Farrell, who stands outside the queue examining his badge.

'Ha-ha, Pete's alright until you get on the wrong side of him. Broke a lad's jaw last year, Quirke's brother reckons,' Farrell says.

Now we travel down a long corridor, past glass-topped walls and lines of framed photos of students receiving trophies. We pass a tall door at the foot of a stairs, where Peter F. Shylock and Mac stand, looking through Mac's blue folder. Peter F. Shylock looks up, seeming to see all of us at once, like the *Mona Lisa*.

We walk down two flights of stairs and come into a long battered looking corridor. There is a chill in the air as we enter the prefabs.

'Welcome to hell,' Quirke says.

The prefect opens the door of room ten and we file in with some others from a nearby village. Quirke sits in the second row with Farrell and O'Brien and I take the last seat. Melvin sits near the back with a thin boy he seems to know already.

The classroom is the same dull beige colour of the corridor, with thin lighting tubes on the ceiling. The cardboard-like walls are scratched with names and initials, parts of the covering have been scraped off, revealing a nucleus of chipboard. To one side, there are square pigeon holes for school bags. To the other, glass panels look out on a grey expanse of yard with small sections of grass before a long short wall. There are steps leading up to a higher fenced area which seems to be tennis courts with most of the nets missing. Further on, there are trees in a sort of sparse wood. Grey

16

pebble-dashed walls present the main building to the left. I see a large block faced building to the far right.

This room is to be our home for the next nine months. The school and grounds, our residence for the next five years. Quirke explains the geography of the area. Beyond the partition in front is room eleven, a Second Year nest. Behind, the banging, shouting and jeering, signifies room nine, another First Year class. Further down the corridor is room eight, also home to First Years.

I straighten out my green copies on the desk. Mam had written my name across the bottom on each one.

A girl with long blonde hair sits in front of us. She checks her copies, while I admire her tresses.

'Something wrong with the jaw, Brush?' Farrell says, elbowing me in the ribs. 'Do you fancy Rebecca?'

I close my mouth and feel my cheeks going red.

Rebecca looks back suddenly for a second. She has very round, blue eyes. She returns to her copies. I notice her beauty more now, feeling a warmth in my abdomen.

Mac arrives at the door, holding his blue folder.

'Hey, hey,' he says. 'Room Ten. Very good. Okay, listen here for your timetable, if you would put it into your homework diaries.'

There are a lot of 'Double Irish' and 'Double maths' which I am a bit worried about, but nevertheless science should be interesting, art and even music. I have never really got to grips with any instrument but the thought of playing in the school band was exciting.

The first teacher at 9.50 is a man of about sixty, with shiny, greased down hair, wrinkles and a check suit.

'Fogarty,' Quirke confirms. 'Piece of piss.' Mr Fogarty spends the whole class shaking hands with each pupil and welcoming them to the school. He asks about their particular village, what age they are, despite almost everyone being thirteen, and what they are looking forward to for the year. He gets a variety of answers, some more accommodating than others.

Mr Fogarty teaches Irish. I only discover this at the end of the class, when he mutters something about it near the blackboard.

'He's lovely,' Orla says, a blonde girl wearing glasses, who sits beside Rebecca.

The English teacher, Mrs Morahan is a small dumpy woman of perhaps forty. She asks each of us what our ambition is and I volunteer my interest in becoming a journalist.

'Where would you like to work?' she says.

'I don't know. One of the newspapers, I suppose.'

'Good man!' Mrs Morahan says. 'Anyone else want to work in journalism or literature?' The class is silent. 'What about you, eh – Arnold?'

Melvin moves in his seat.

'Are you okay?'

He grunts a response. I could have told her Melvin had only one interest. He's never hidden the fact that all he ever wanted to do was take over his elderly father's farm. The only thing that stands in his way is one of his older brothers, Dominic, who has similar aspirations.

The big novelty about secondary school is the three breaks. We'd always had just two in the village school. The first is at 10.45. We don't know what to do with ourselves and

18

sit talking at our desks. The thin boy that Melvin seems to know is Conway. I recognise him now from a few inter school matches. He lives quite near Melvin but went to a different primary school.

The next teacher is Mr O'Leary who seems friendly and teaches maths. By noon, I am getting hungry. I look forward to the lunch mam packed for me. She said she would put a few things extra as it was the first day. A tall figure enters the room swiftly, stops at the table and swings round. I hear Quirke mutter 'Sharpe,' to Farrell.

It seems Mrs Sharpe heard Quirke too.

'You, lad, are you saying something?'

Quirke looks up, his skin matching the colour of his neat red fringe.

'No, miss,' he says.

'My name is Mrs Sharpe. I am teaching Geography. Start taking the following down…' There was a flurry of books and desks opening. 'Over the course we will be…'

She launched into about fifteen minutes of geographical terminology I could not understand and I doubt anyone else could.

'Now, I have to discuss some school-related business with you, class. I am responsible for pupil uniformity and general appearance. There will be an official inspection at the end of next week and the last Friday of every month thereafter. However, I can already inform some of you that you are in breach of regulations.'

Mrs Sharpe looks along the front row.

'You girl, those earrings. I don't want to see them again.'

Orla goes a deep red.

'You, girl down there, with red hair. Those rings on your fingers. Have them removed.' She made it sound like they were moles. She turns back to the table. Then she looks straight at me.

'You, man. What are you going to do with that?' She twitches her head a minute distance, but it is clear she is focussing on my ponytail. I drop the multi-coloured biro Mam had bought.

'You can brainstorm in different colours,' she had said and laughed, as she handed it to me with a lot of other things for my pencil case.

The biro makes a loud clack on the desk.

I find I cannot speak.

'Well? You will cut it off by the weekend.' Mrs Sharpe nods to me.

My throat is dry. Mrs Sharpe has moved on to someone else, but her words just melt into a blur. My face is red as I absorb the words 'cut it off' again and again in my mind.

'Hey, Brush? Brush? Are you still with us?' Farrell says. The class is over. Mrs Sharpe is gone.

My appetite has vanished. I look at the ham sandwiches Mam has wrapped in cling film and the yoghurt with little enthusiasm. 'Cut it off.'

After we have eaten, we venture as far as the end of the corridor. We are still a bit shy to really investigate the school. Hundreds of blue-clad figures mill around outside, shouting, throwing a ball in groups, the girls and boys fairly well segregated. Two tall boys are in a headlock and drag each other around in a circle on the yard to low jeering.

Mr O'Leary is standing on an elevated patch of grass, reading a newspaper.

'O'Leary is on yard duty,' Quirke confirms. 'Sure we'll

have a nose about.'

We village boys move en masse, Quirke and Farrell leading the way, me and Melvin behind, new associate Conway in a kind of hybrid position between us, with O'Brien holding up the rear.

We walk towards the cluster of trees at the end of a winding dirt track. I notice smaller groups of students amongst the narrow trunks, mostly older than us, but there are a few First Years. They look up, their eyes dart around, toward the prefabs and at the large pebble dash of the main building.

'What's going on in there?' I say. Quirke and Farrell make a sound like I asked a silly question.

'Faggin'. What else? No lookout at the path – that I saw anyway. They'll learn,' Quirke says.

'What? They're smoke–,'

'Shush!' Quirke says. 'Jesus, do you want Pete to hear ya?'

'But are they smoking? I thought it wasn't allowed,' I whisper.

Farrell and Quirke laugh horrifically. 'Ah, Brush,' Farrell says.

'How are ye lads?' It is a voice amongst the trees. Two tall boys emerge, their badges announce them as Carvey and Needham. I can smell the tar as they approach. Their skin is pale, I imagine already dulled from nicotine.

'What are ye at?' Farrell says. It seems they have all met already, unbeknownst to me.

'Down there, having an old smoke,' Needham says, with a hint of a maniacal tone. Carvey coughs deeply, as though to confirm it.

'What if ye get caught?' I say.

'We won't get caught, unless you squeal.' Carvey stands over me. He is at least four inches taller. He eyes me. I wait for my village associates to spring to my defence but no one does anything. Farrell looks at Needham, Quirke chews gum, Melvin plays with his balls. O'Brien actually looks worried.

'What's that?' Carvey says, his twitching motion is quite similar to Mrs Sharpe's. I guess he is talking about my ponytail.

'What?' I say, noticing a little shake in my voice.

'That'll have to go,' Needham says, turning to me.
'Clip-clip!' He makes a cutting gesture.

They stand over me now, like towers. A warm ball of something turns in my stomach.

'Hey, hey,' Mac shouts from somewhere. I am relieved. Mac waves his blue folder. Carvey and Needham are gone. I look down at the groups of smokers, but they have vanished, the leaves flicker in the breeze.

'Let's go, break's over,' Mac says. 'Hey, hey.'

On the way back in, we slow at room eight, the pace set as usual by Quirke. 'How ya Tommy?' Quirke says to someone within whom he knows from football apparently. Room ten is quite well behaved, but room eight is machinelike. Everyone is already in their seats, patiently awaiting 1.50 and the next class. Even the 'Tommy' Quirke hailed is reluctant to engage in much of a conversation. Only at the back, there is one boy chatting with two quite pretty girls. I take in the other students as we lounge around the door, enjoying the feeling of superiority, the slightly less conformable status our slow return to class is giving us. Along the back row, there is a large stout boy with terrible acne, a flat-faced character with snow white hair and an extremely small pupil in between them.

'Come on, we better go,' Quirke says.

Carvey and Needham are standing outside room nine. 'Lads, lads, what's the panic on ye?' Needham says. We don't stop at room nine, mainly because there are so many objects flying through the air, there is every chance one would find its way through the doorway and strike us in the eye. I see chairs and desks are up-ended, some of the class are involved in a wrestling competition. I am somewhat relieved to get back to the relative calm of room ten.

The next teacher is Miss Tuohy, who teaches French. She does not appear to be overly enthused about this and lays out the syllabus in a fairly inanimate manner.

The afternoon goes fairly quickly. The last break finds pupils at a more wakened state. Melvin is the strongest of our band and it has been noticed by the other First Years. Apparently, possible scrap pairings have already been pre-selected, Quirke reports.

'There's a fella in room eight called Keadin, you could give him a bit of a going over to try out,' Quirke is saying to Melvin as we pack up, at the end of the first day. 'Then you'd be ready to take on Carvey.'

What's this about? I didn't know Melvin was going scrapping. I don't want to bring attention to my ignorance, so I try to listen in.

'You take Carvey down, you'll rule First Year.'

'Keadin's mate Ryan was up, trying to set it for last break Friday.'

'Would you be on, Melv?'

'What, sure I don't know this Keadin or Ryan. I don't know them lads down there at all,' Melvin says.

'You don't need to know him, Melv, you just need to scrap him,' Farrell says.

'Ryan is the fella who was chatting to the women. Keadin is the big fat lad in the back. That dwarf beside is Murphy and the fella with the head like a shovel is Keegan, he's a mountainy sheep farmer,' Quirke says briskly.

'Why don't you scrap him?' Melvin says. For a man that didn't say a lot he could certainly talk his way out of things when he needed to.

'I'd look nice,' Quirke says, looking down at his chest, perhaps trying to create an expression that represented his size.

Bags packed and we head out the corridor, up the steps, back through the main building, along with the hordes of others, toward the entrance porch. In front of me, there is a tall boy with fair hair to his shoulders. He is in Fourth Year or Leaving Cert and wears a small earring. Farrell gives me a push.

'Come on Brush, get a move on.'

'Ouch, get off Farrell.'

Giddy, I exaggerate Farrell's nudge and run against the fair-haired boy. He looks around.

24

'Eh, sorry,' I smile. 'It was his fault,' I nod toward Farrell, but he has hurried past.

The fair-haired boy bites his lip. Knuckles ram my crotch. The pain comes in dull powerful waves. The fair-haired boy is gone. I keep walking, despite the surge in my abdomen.

I get on the bus, the pain having reached a crescendo. O'Brien pushes me down the aisle toward the end.

'First Years no further back then the fifth seat from the end,' Lordan, a Second Year, tells us, 'or ye'll be lugged out.'

I sit beside Melvin, the pain finally subsiding. After two minutes, there is a tug on my ponytail. I look around. Three First Years behind look placidly ahead, one of them Conway. I turn back. Ponytail pulled again, this time harder. I turn around again. Same scene. I slowly look ahead. Ponytail pulled again. I look around, no clues. I look ahead. I swing back a few seconds later. Everyone stares blankly.

'What are you looking at?' a deep voice shouts from the back. I look forward. Ponytail pulled again. I act like I didn't feel anything. I look at Melvin, he stares dreamily ahead. Farrell and Quirke across the aisle could not be guilty, O'Brien, behind them, looks out the window. I look forward. Ponytail pulled again. I act like I didn't feel anything. Ponytail pulled again. Hard, like the hair would be pulled out. I look around instantly. Absolutely no clues.

Lordan comes to my shoulder. 'Marcus said if you look around again, you're dead.'

'Who's Marcus?'

Lordan smiles nightmarishly. 'He's a Leaving Cert. The Daddy. If he sees you doing that again, he'll kill you.'

'The Daddy?'

'He runs the place. He's sound. Last year The Daddy we had made all the First Years pay ten p a week security.'

'Security?'

'Yeah – from not getting your head kicked.'

'But someone keeps pulling my hair.'

'Just ignore it. Good lad.'

Lordan goes back to his seat four rows from the end. I sit back, contemplating the underground control systems I have just learned of, when my ponytail is pulled again.

'For God's sake!' I say. I glance across at Quirke.

'Don't look back, whatever you do,' he says sagely.

Ponytail pulled again, very hard. I push my head against the back of the seat. This is not easy to do, as the seat does not have a very tall back rest and I have to slide very low to get my ponytail out of the target zone. I stare resolutely at the back of the seat in front.

Mam has the dinner on the table when I get home. I am so hungry, I can barely tell her about the day. Dad had said it would be a bit different going to secondary school and I can see now how right he was. It is after dinner I tell mam about the incident with Mrs Sharpe. She says she will write a letter to the school about it. Somewhat relieved, I go to my bedroom, take out the new homework diary in my room and peruse its advisory notes.

Apparently, the pupil should spend four hours per night at homework. Six pm to ten pm is the recommended time. Not much room for TV then. I enjoy reading the advice, to take a break with a cup of tea or a cold drink every hour, a brisk walk outside before study. Then I realise it is already half past seven and I have not started the homework. I begin to think about what I should do next, when there is a knock on the window.

The green woollen cap signifies it is Doyle. I open the window.

'How's tricks?' he says, climbing in, in his usual fashion.

'What's the craic?' I say, as he lands on my bed and dives to the obsolete armchair I procured when we got some new furniture in the sitting room. 'How did you get on above?'

'Oh, you know all about that place. Don't know what I'm doing still there. Still had good oul' craic with Old Bubble. Set off the fire extinguisher, meself and McNulty.'

'Did ye?'

'Yeah, Bubble went berserk trying to find out who did it. Then we tied down the boot of his car. Should have seen him this evening trying to get his bags in, ha-ha! Didn't do a thing. Dossing all day.'

I knock on the Bush television, also formerly in loftier positions of the house and lie back on the bed.

'Ah yes, we'd some craic. I'll do fuck all this year now. I know it all anyway,' Doyle continues.

'But you'd want to do a bit, isn't that why you stayed back?'

Doyle looks up, his face colouring a little. 'No, I was well up with ye. I'm not slow. It was the age, Bubble tol' th' oul' lady. See I'm six months younger than you and Skeletor.'

The old nicknames seem to have faded from memory in the hullaballoo of the new adventure in secondary school. Mine of course would never die, but Melvin's rhythmic connection to the evil cartoon character Skeletor could easily dissolve into the sea of teenage life.

Quirke had been linked to *Quincy*, a television programme about a doctor and his calling card had become Doc. Farrell's father walked like a duck so it was said, so the questionable honour was bestowed on him. O'Brien, having reportedly sat on some margarine in the distant memory of the infant classroom had grown up with the horrifically satisfying 'Butterarse'. Only mine was used as a term of endearment. The others were highly insulting and never used in direct speech, particularly Doyle's Hogget, a reference to his father's extensive sheep farming activities. In very hostile altercations it was adapted to 'Hoggy.'

'Yeah, I'll fly through it. What's it's like down in that place? Ducked ye into toilets, yet?'

'Nah. Nothing like that. Fierce amount of work, though.'

'What work? Sure don't bother doing it.'

'The diary says you're meant to do four hours a night.'

'Four hours a night? Ha-ha! Some chance. Are you gonna be a doctor or something?'

'I was thinking of journalism.'

'Ha-ha. Right. Did you see the bike?'

Doyle leads me out through the window into the cool night air. He has a flash lamp he carries everywhere and directs it against his BMX.

'I found a can of silver paint in the shed. Said I'd give it a bit of a facelift.'

'So you did.' Doyle had completely covered the bike in the silver paint. 'Nice job, nice job.'

'Yeah. Like a new bike,' Doyle says, happily.

'Did you get bit on your hands?' I say, noticing the somewhat unusual colour of his skin.

'What? I painted it yesterday?'

Then I see through the window, the armchair has a long silver track across its cushion.

'It's not dry, yet?' Doyle says, urgently. The back of his green jacket is silver at the bottom.

'Is that the stuff for heating pipes? It's maybe not for this type of metal, Doyler?' I say.

'I'm going,' Doyle says.

'See you later,' I say, as he disappears with the silver BMX. What an eejit.

Even though I am whacked tired, I cannot sleep for ages. The images of the day play and play again in my head. There is the yellow bus, with the branches scraping the roof, Mad-Dog swerving, me banging my head against the iron bar, the new faces of Carvey, Needham, Ryan, Keadin, Keegan, Murphy and now Mann, Corless, Houston, Conway, Rebecca appear, the warnings of Peter F. Shylock, the introductions of Mr Fogarty, Mrs Morahan, Mr O'Leary, Miss Tuohy. The dream becomes a nightmare and combined images of Mrs Sharpe and the fair-haired Fourth Year flash, one pulling my ponytail, the other punching me in the testicles, Mac saying 'Hey, hey!', waving his blue folder over the whole fracas, and finally Doyle cycling into the scene on his sticky silver BMX, headlong into Marley and O'Toole.

I wake up a bit late, half seven was the time Dad had advised and I had been up at seven that first morning. This morning it's twenty to eight, and I hurriedly gobble some cornflakes. Mad-dog doesn't bother much about the ticket today, just a cursive glance. The journey too seems quicker, I am further down the bus, sitting next to Melvin again, who is dozing. No one is in the mood for play-acting on the way, people are still waking up.

There is no assembly today and we file straight down toward room ten.

In the corridor as we walk along, I see the fair-haired Fourth Year coming. I look to the floor, hoping he will not notice me. Just as he is passing and I breathe out, his left hand flies across and squeezes my testicles hard. The pain brings tears to my eyes. It is almost completely gone by the first break, over an hour and a half later.

The classes begin to move by quicker. Mrs Morahan is back, dispensing a ton of homework, Mr O'Leary launches into his syllabus. At breaks, we gather at the prefab entrance. The Leaving Certs wander around the yard, or through the tennis courts, kicking a ball at each other. Quirke knows them through his brother and informs us of their names and nicknames, but there are so many, I only remember the ones from our bus. Sometimes, there is some chat with others, often Mann, Corless and Houston stop on their way to the woods for a quick fag. They are all smokers, since primary school, it seems. Quirke usually leads the conversation with these outsiders.

When Mann comes, he has an unnerving habit of jabbing people in the ribs. The first morning he does this, Farrell jabs him back, Quirke dances out of his way, Skeletor also returns the tap. Mann butts his knuckles in my side, it looked softer than it was. For some reason I do not hit back, just laugh it off, smiling.

'Y'alright there Brush?' Mann says, as if he knows me very well.

'Ha-ha,' I say, trying to seem intimidating.

When Mann's crew are gone, Farrell turns to me. 'You should have hit that fat cunt back, Brush, what's wrong with ya?'

'Can't let them away with that shite,' Quirke says.

'Didn't feel anything,' I murmur.

By Wednesday, I have more or less settled into a routine. I sleep well Tuesday night, and get up at twenty to eight next morning. The ponytail pervert is still active, so I position my head low, pressed to the back of the seat. Sometimes I forget and get a good tug. There are three suspects behind me. Conway and the Moran twins are definite possibilities. James, or Jimmy as he prefers to be known, smokes and talks loudly to an inter cert sitting across the aisle next to O'Brien. In the middle, his brother Joseph stares stonily ahead. Out of the three I suspect Jimmy. Lordan and Quirke's brother sit further back, but it would be difficult for them to sit back down quickly enough. But even if I catch any of them, it's not like I can sit behind them, or turn permanently around. So I eventually conclude attaching the back of my head to the seat is the only current solution.

I continue this first week to admire Rebecca Joyce. I steal glances at her blue eyes, her sallow skin and her white teeth. I

31

wonder about how to talk to her. This is as far I can get with this problem at present.

On Thursday morning, all the First Years are called to the assembly hall. A number of teachers stand behind tables along the windows. Most of these teachers I have not seen before. It is the day for choosing our optional subjects, Quirke confirms. I have been looking forward to this. There is a problem though. Melvin wants to do woodwork and I want to do German. Melvin wants to do mechanical drawing and I want to do art.

'What are you doing that oul' shite for?' Quirke says.

'That oul' art, sure it's just oul' fannies at that craic,' O'Brien puts in.

'Yeah, nancies. Come on down to the woodshed, Brush, it'll be good craic,' Farrell concludes.

Only Melvin does not offer an opinion. He stands against the long radiator under the enormous windows, twiddling his thick fingers and looking around the hall uncomfortably.

'Are ye near ready for the second cut?' he will only say to Conway. It eventually transpires that Melvin was helping Conway with bringing in hay earlier in the summer.

'Nearly. That 10-10-20 is great stuff, the way the grass comes up.'

'It's hard work, the hay,' I say.

'Not too bad, if you're organised,' Conway says.

'That trailer ye have is a great yoke,' Melvin says to Conway.

'What sort of tractor do ye have?' I say.

32

'Zetor,' Conway says.

'Yeah, the exact same as us. Good machine,' Melvin says. 'How do ye find the p.t.o.?'

'That's the drive, is it?' I say.

'Hey, hey,' Mac says as he arrives in the hall with his blue folder. 'Now have you all selected the two optional subjects you want and registered?'

A couple of prefects move around the hall nudging First Years in various directions.

'You lad,' one says to me. 'Are you with these guys?' Quirke, Farrell, and O'Brien join Melvin and Conway who walk toward a teacher who holds a large saw in his hand.

'Why did he bring the saw with him?' Needham says, as he brushes past with Carvey. 'Like lads – this is what ye use in Woodwork – like doh – thanks for clearing that up!'

'Ye never know Needle, he might forget what his job is,' Carvey says.

The prefect stands in front of me awaiting a response. My friends have moved a distance away now. Beside the woodwork table is a desk with some wooden T-Squares. The woodwork teacher teaches mechanical drawing as well.

'I'm going for journalism,' I tell the prefect.

He opens and closes his mouth. I note he is wearing a brace. 'I didn't ask ya what you're going for, I asked what subjects are you picking, now come on, we don't want to be here all day.'

I watch Melvin and Conway laugh about something. O'Brien is discussing one of the saws at the woodwork teacher's table with Farrell and Quirke. I look around. Near a piano in the corner, a small German flag is laid on a table in front of a petite woman. Some flat-headed room eight pupils hover nearby. There is also a girl with golden hair chewing gum. The art table is in front of the stage. A moustachioed man stands regimentally behind it, arms folded, staring ahead. I see one lanky boy from room nine and a few other girls there.

'Can you change your mind?' I ask the prefect.

'Change – Ugh! No – not really,' the prefect says.

'I don't know what –,'

'Just pick your subject and get on, everyone else is gone now, for God's sake.'

I am now one of the few remaining students in the centre of the hall, apart from a girl who seems to be crying and Houston, who sits on a chair, asleep.

'Can you do art and woodwork?' I say.

The prefect consults a sheet. 'No,' he says.

'What about German and woodwork, I want to study journalism, you see–'

'No.'

'Art and mechanical drawing?'

'Look laddin', do they sound like they go together? Rulers and paintbrushes?'

'Hey, hey, is there a problem, here?' Mac waves his blue folder.

'This lad doesn't know what he's doing, sir.'

'It's okay Henry, I'll take care of this.'

'Grump!' I hear the prefect say quietly, walking away, as though exasperated beyond all conceivability.

'Hey, what's the problem?'

34

'I'm going doing journalism, sir, and I wasn't sure whether art and German might be the right choice instead of woodwork and mechanical drawing.'

'Oh, yes, art and German,' Mac says with some assurance. 'German would be useful for journalism, now off you go there.'

I walk across the hall, in the corner of my eye I can see my village friends in a group talking. I arrive at the art table and sign my name. I walk over to the German table.

There, the golden-haired girl chewing gum turns around, smiles at me and hands me the sheet. She has brown eyes. On her badge, her name reads Alannah.

'Hi,' she says.

'Thanks,' I say. She smiles. I sign my name and hand it back to her. I feel the skin of her hand against mine. Then I walk back to my village friends who are gravitating toward the back of the assembly hall.

Despite Peter F. Shylock's warnings about smoking not being permitted anywhere, it is soon clear the use of tobacco is widespread in almost every hidden corner of the school and fairly openly on the bus. The journey home is in fact much different to the mornings, the students are awake, hungry and giddy. Quirke's brother and Lordan wrestle with each other. A tall thin Fourth Year, discreetly referred to as The Weasel, catapults precisely targeted folded cards, loaded with pennies for greater impact, up the aisle at a range of angled buttocks.

I sit again with my head pushed against the back of the seat.

'Did ye open the pit yet?' Melvin asks.

'Not yet,' I say. Dad says I can feed the cattle on Saturdays and Sundays this year when they are housed for the winter. I know Melvin has already begun machine milking his father's cows.

'Was it treble chop or double chop?' Melvin continues.

I try to think of an answer which does not betray my lack of knowledge. The day of the silage cutting was long and boring, I was stationed at the edge of the growing mound of freshly chopped grass in the yard, trimming the edges with a grape.

As I sit up, in the thrust of the conversation, my ponytail is pulled from behind. I look around instinctively.

Jimmy pulls on a cigarette, Joseph stares stonily ahead, Conway, on the inside, looks dreamily out the window.

'What are you looking at?' Marcus roars. I turn back.

Lordan arrives beside me. 'You're on your last warning,' he says. 'You're pissing off The Daddy. First Years can't look back the aisle. It's the rules. There are penalties.' His breath smells of cheese and onion crisps, and I am starving.

'They'll bring you down there, and then you'll know it,' Quirke says from across the aisle. 'You better watch yourself, Brush.'

'They're cutting hay in there,' Melvin says, looking out at a passing field of knocked grass. 'Risky this week, I'd say,' he adds, nodding to the gathering clouds. 'I suppose you have to cut it sometime. You can't put it off forever.'

'Are you milking now every evening?' I say, affably. As Melvin nods, my ponytail is pulled again. I turn my head sideways and look down through the narrow space between the seats. No movement behind. Further on, Quirke's brother and Lordan chat. Across the aisle Farrell and Quirke could not do it. Behind them is just O'Brien, who sits next to a … a schoolbag, is all I can see. Some of the back row crew probably took a seat for their bag.

It is impossible to relax, as every time I lift my head, my hair is pulled. I cannot look back or look forward. All I can do is sit with my head flat against the seat.

'What are you at, Brush?' Farrell says, noticing my odd posture.

'Some bastard keeps pulling me hair,' I say.

'Cut it off,' Farrell advises.

Slap on the head now. I dare not look up. The top of my head stings. I look over at Melvin who laughs.

'They'll soon forget about ya,' he says, with a consoling tone. 'That's a big Zetor, isn't it?'

That's what Mrs Sharpe had said. Cut it off.

I make a serious plan to get all the assigned homework done that evening. But after dinner, I am so tired I just want to lie on the couch and watch *Home and Away* and then *Minder*. At seven I take out my books at the kitchen table.

English, I have to write a short composition. Simple enough. I write about a boy who cannot sit normally on his school bus because other pupils keep slapping him on the head. Irish, ten sentences have to be written, it is difficult and boring. Maths, I lost concentration when Mr O'Leary was explaining how to find the 'probability of simple events'. I was looking at Rebecca Joyce. I do the problems, but I guess they are wrong. History – Mac teaches this subject, down in the bowels of the really old part of the school, still mostly untouched since its days as a nun's convent.

I like it down there, for some reason, despite everyone complaining about the dampness, the bad light, the musty smell. Actually, I particularly like the musty smell. The old caretaker, Packie, seems to spend most of his time walking up and down its mysterious corridors, carrying a brush.

Mac had introduced us to primitive man and the various utensils he had invented to make life easier. The stone was the vital raw material. Hunting axes are one implement I recall his goatee-surrounded mouth explaining. We must answer questions relating to the chapter on hunting utensils. I cannot find an answer to a question, the back of my neck stings.

My mind is full of things and I cannot concentrate. I write a few lines, with the sinking knowledge it is not what he is looking for. He never checks the homework anyway, I notice, not like in the village school where everything was scrutinized and you would be kept in at lunchtime if it was wrong. There are four more subjects to do. I take a deep breath. It is after ten when I finish. The homework diary was right.

I imagine the five years ahead of this. Five years of fours hours every night.

Actually it gets harder, we have been told, after First Year. How many more hours are there in the evenings? Some students spend their Saturdays studying, Mam says.

I do not sleep that well.

Friday in the school has a different atmosphere. Students seem excited about the weekend, there are more smiles, conversations are louder, books are not gripped as tightly. Even the teachers seem to take today's lessons less seriously. Apart from Mrs Sharpe. She has not mentioned my choice of hairstyle since. Peter F. Shylock will have gotten mam's letter by now. She simply glances at me sourly, as she explains concepts of water irrigation at breakneck speed.

I have my first German lesson. The boys in the class look peculiar, they have odd hairstyles: afros and Elvis type crew-cuts. Alannah sits at the front. I sit next to her. I spend the class trying to get my elbow to collide with hers. She looks at me at one stage, I am fairly sure I saw this at the side of my eye. The teacher tells us how to say 'hello' in German, but I have forgotten it later.

My art class mates are similarly absurd. A gangly collector of Tipex bottles known as 'Bendy' sits next to me, across from a group of perennially giggling girls. Most bizarre is the teacher, a Mr Kirk, who scratches his moustache repeatedly to the point of it becoming a major irritation to any witness. He is obsessed with three boxes behind his table, where he spends most of the lesson in the unheated art room, pausing only to glare at the guffawing girls, before resuming his mysterious search.

At lunchtime, the woodwork class discuss their experiences.

'He's good on the saw,' Conway is saying.

'Class,' Farrell agrees.

'See the Tenon he did,' O'Brien adds.

I try to seem enthused by their remarks despite having only portraiture and subjectivity to offer them in return.

Rebecca turns to us. She has a pot of creamed rice, a slick silver pouch of orange and an expensive looking bagel for lunch. She glances at my bread and butter sandwich and digestive biscuit, my Roughneck flask of lukewarm tea.

Mam's enthusiasm for elaborate lunch packs seems to have waned.

'Do you have a ruler?' she says to me.

'No,' I reply shortly, feeling heat on my face.

'Oh,' she says, pausing, and then turning back to her bagel and her conversation with Orla, which is generally interspersed with loud giggles.

We stand at the double doors of the large grey building, known as the 'Complex' and used for sports. Within are dressing rooms and a large wooden floor sports surface. P.E. starts next week, Quirke tells us. 'Tuohy teaches it. She's a fucking header,' he says.

Some students use the large size of the Complex to camouflage their tobacco-related activities. I see a group at the far corner, cautiously looking toward the main building for any sign of Mac or Peter F. Shylock.

'What's the football team like here?' Farrell says. He is a star player for the parish.

'What you make of it,' Quirke says simply.

'Yeah, but is it a good set up?'

'Middlin'. One street town like this, you know yourself. Good training, but the First Year coach is meant to be a bit of a dick. I think they made the county quarters last year.'

'Not bad,' Farrell says.

'How's the boys?' Needham says, walking around the corner with Carvey.

'What's the craic?' Carvey says.

'Are you goin' playing football for the First Year team, Carvey?' Farrell says. He stands straight up, but still he is not as tall as Carvey.

'Don't know, lot a hassle,' Carvey growls, catching my eye. I look away. 'Come on, we'll get a quick drag before the bell.'

'Down the corner?' Needham eyes the end of the building.

'Fuck that, let's go into the trees,' Carvey says. 'Too risky over there, they're alright, they're Fourth Years, they don't give a fuck.'

'Ye comin' girls?' Needham looks around at us. While he is as tall as Carvey, he is half the width, he wavers thinly, like a shadow of his associate.

We stand silently.

'None of us smoke,' Farrell announces.

'Health freaks, what? Melvin, are you goin' taking on that fat prick in room eight this evening?' Needham says.

'I don't know,' Melvin says, standing squarely at the door. A snot drips from his nostril.

'Ryan came up a while ago and told us yer man was still up for it,' Quirke puts in. 'We'll be down alright.'

'Prefab cloakroom?' Carvey says.

'Yup.' Quirke nods. 'The brother says Mac doesn't know about it.'

'Doesn't know about it?' O'Brien says. 'How can he not know about it?'

'He doesn't know we use it for scraps,' Farrell says, with some impatience.

'Our man'll fucking kill that fat bastard,' Quirke says.

'It's just a test run, anyway,' I say.

'Test run for what?' Needham says, quickly. Farrell and O'Brien step back. Quirke scowls at me.

'Test run for what, Brush?'

'For whatever,' I say, looking at the little stones around my feet.

Carvey looks at Needham. 'Come on,' Carvey says.

'Hey, that cow, Aine Muldoon reckons she's going out with ya?' Needham says, as he moves away. I realise he is looking at me.

'Who's Aine Muldoon?' I say.

'Yer wan with the face like a pig's stomach.'

'Come on,' Carvey says, walking away from the door. As he passes me, his fist connects with my rib. It is light, but I feel it. I do not react, just looking at him as he walks away, not turning back. Needham reaches his side and speaks to him as they quickly walk toward the trees.

'He'd be a great fielder,' Farrell is saying. My head is mixed up. I stand looking at Carvey and Needham disappearing amongst the greenery, flashes of blue shrinking in the distance.

'Dirty bastard, though, I'd say. You'd want the old cup under the jocks,' Quirke concludes.

After Mr Fogarty completes thirty-five minutes of being completely ignored, the bell goes for the last break at 2.45.

'Come on, Melv, let's go.'

'I'm not going anywhere. Sure I don't even know that fella. I'm staying here. Meself and Conway are having a good talk.' They resume an informed discussion on weed sprays.

'Fuck this, we'll be a laughing stock,' Quirke says. 'We better go down and tell them. Fuck you, Melvin.' Melvin simply smiles.

I walk with Quirke, Farrell and O'Brien to the end of the corridor. The room eight contingent are not much more impressive. Only Ryan and Keegan are actually in the cloakroom. Murphy leans against the door.

'Look lads,' Ryan says, sounding like a TV presenter. 'Our man has jacked. He actually went home a while ago. He's from town. I don't know. Sorry.'

'No bother,' says Quirke quickly. 'Let's arrange it for next week.'

'Where is Melvin, anyway?' Keegan says. His extremely deep voice sounds like dad, if not granda.

'Yeah, yeah, he's comin' but I'll tell him it's off,' Quirke says, edging away.

'Where's the big scrap?' Needham booms, arriving with Carvey. I notice Mann and his crew coming behind.

A fist lands in my testicles. Swinging blond hair flashes amongst a passing group of Fourth Years.

'No scrap today,' Ryan says, officially, as I try to halt the urge to kneel and bend over.

'Times up, anyway,' Farrell says, looking at his watch.

'That's the trouble with these test fights,' Needham says, looking at me. I get a fist in the stomach as Mann brushes past. Houston laughs as though someone has told a joke in his head.

'You need to have a good fucking reason to scrap. Then they'll show up,' Needham says.

I have mixed feelings at the end of the first week. I go to bed quite early Friday night. I have a ton of homework. Mr Kirk has even given us written exercises on top of history, geography, commerce, maths, English, Irish, German and French. There is no time to enjoy the introductory chapter to the sciences as I have so many other things to do. I decide to leave them until Sunday. Saturday, I help dad on the farm. We usually bring my grandparents on dad's side to Mass on Saturday evening. Mam's dad died years ago, her mother is bedridden and lives with us. Gran doesn't go to Mass anymore, even though she'd probably like to. I don't see her much, once a day at the most if I bring her a beaker of tea and a few biscuits. She hardly eats anything nowadays. Doyle comes with his BMX on Sunday, newly restored to its rusting blue and red.

'It took my three hours to wash off that bloody silver paint,' he says.

Some is still on his sleeve. We examine the re-modified bicycle. Doyle has attached a large radio to the handlebars.

'Turned it on full blast, comin' down the road,' Doyle says. 'Oul' Heneghan was looking out the window! "Bleddy hooligan" he said, imagine!'

'Jesus, you'd want to watch it,' I say. 'That fella would ring the guards.'

'For what?' Doyle says, climbing in my window.

'For disturbing the peace probably,' I say, as I follow him in.

'Arrah, who cares,' Doyle mutters. He takes off his woollen cap and settles on the armchair. Mam had managed to clean off most of the silver paint.

'What's on the oul' box tonight?' Doyle says.

We have two channels wired to the bedroom and the choice is limited. '*Minder* is on UTV but we can't see it here,' I say apologetically.

'D'ya want to fire up th' oul' SEGA?' Doyle says.

I groan to myself, getting the SEGA Mega Drive off the shelf. This will be at least a three hour visit now, as Doyle, once he starts playing, cannot stop until he exhausts all of Sonic the hedgehog's lives trying to get through Green Hill Zone. It's Sunday night, and the morning won't be long coming, I don't want to be wrecked tired.

'Any chance of a cup?' Doyle says, clicking on the games console.

The mornings are a relief on the bus from the evening ritual of ponytail pulling which I fear is going to carry on through the winter. I am no closer to identifying the culprit. The prohibition on turning my head around has proved something of a handicap in my investigations. Assembly is called again on Monday. This is unusual, Quirke confirms.

We line up in the large hall, knowing our positions now. There is a different, more muted feel to this morning in the hall, the expectation and excitement of a week ago dulled now, perhaps by the realisation the secondary school experience involves work, hopeless inflammation of hormones and intimidation.

'Good morning,' Peter F. Shylock booms as he takes his position in centre stage. Mac stands near the wing

45

scratching his goatee. 'It appears that my words last week have gone unheeded. As I outlined then, smoking is completely prohibited in the school or on the grounds. This rule also applies to pupils on their way to and from the school. Despite this, I have already dealt with a number of offenders who now face very strict penalties. Let this be a warning to the rest of you. Anyone found to be smoking within these areas will be severely dealt with. Teachers have also brought to my attention some negligence in carrying out homework assignments. This is unacceptable. Homework must be completed in full and delivered on time. This stipulation is in force from day one, not the week before the Christmas tests. Anyone not complying with this will face strict penalties. I do not expect to repeat myself on this matter for the term.'

While Peter F. Shylock speaks, a faint murmur of twittering has broken out. It fades quickly, no one wants The Principal to pick them out. Nevertheless, there has certainly been an incident of some kind up the lines. I strain my head to see. Quirke is laughing to himself at the back. Despite being miles from the action, he seemed to know about it before me.

'What happened?' I say to Melvin. Melvin simply responds with his usual 'Don't know.'

I see Orla up at the top, her face is blotchy. Mac is looking down the line. He looks perplexed, as though he has telepathically received a message from space. He returns again to the safety of his blue folder.

Peter F. Shylock booms past the disturbance and continues outlining the rules and regulations of the school, in case anyone missed them last week. When he safely disappears from sight, muttering and giggles begin to break out. As the years are led out of the assembly hall, a group of girls crowd around Orla. I notice a small puddle on the wood floor.

'She pissed herself,' laughs O'Brien, as he bounds past.

'Pissybed!' Needham shouts.

'Pissybed! Pissybed!' a few other room nine members join in as the chant grows.

'Pissybed! Pissybed! Pissybed!' Orla sits on a step at the stage, a handkerchief at her nose, two other girls sit either side. Needham shouts 'Pissybed' to the ceiling as he and a group run past, breaking out of the row. 'You'll be punished for that, line-breaking, boyo!' a prefect shouts.

I look at the puddle as I walk past. It is definitely urine. Orla's skirt is stained. I hear her sniffing as I reach the door. There are still a good twenty First Years behind me and a clear chant of 'Pissybed!' continues. Orla looks up, catches my eye, I adopt the expression I imagine people use at funerals, a kind of sober sympathy.

As we walk out past the entrance doors and down toward room ten, talk is all about Orla.

'Pissin' in Assembly, for fuck's sake!'

'Women, Jaysus Christ!'

'Shut up you fuckin tosser!' This is one of the more fiery females of room nine, Agatha, defined features, curly hair and much taller than me. 'You've nawthin' to piss with!'

Agatha slaps, who I now discover to be Needham, across the face. Blood spills from his cheek.

'Cut yer nails, ya fuckin' dog,' Needham says and walks off, dabbing his cheek with the sleeve of his jumper.

Along the corridor at rooms thirteen to seventeen where the Fourth Years and Leaving Certs reside, I grimly notice the fair haired Fourth Year, identified by Quirke as

47

Martin Ainsworth, lounging at the doorway. He laughs with an inter cert, Frederick Fanning, who I recognise from our bus. Fanning's brother is Maurice The Daddy, and it seems Freddy is The Son and can fraternise with the senior years of the school. The traffic is moving very quickly, they may not notice me.

I keep my head toward the ground as we near them. I hear Martin Ainsworth snigger. Only he could possess a laugh of such despicable sharpness. A finger and a thumb reach out, grip my left nipple and squeeze very hard, before disappearing out of sight. The pain had not even registered at the end of the corridor, but when it does, it lasts for the whole of French class.

I get on the bus early that evening and get a chance to see all the Leaving Certs take their positions without fear of observational-related retribution. Cigar Carr, with thick stubble around his jaw sits in the far left of the back row. Tall and thin like a cat, the Mancunian, Paul Sands passes, jabbing a pencil deep in the thigh of Jimmy Moran, who howls.

'You owe me a fag, you little prick,' Sands snipes. I doubt it is a legitimate claim. I calculate the Leaving Cert smokers demand free tobacco from Jimmy, whose father owns a shop.

'Crazy' Anthony Lafferty prances down the bus, carrying a large cardboard sign with 'Anti-Apartheid' and 'Free Nelson Mandela' written in thick black insulating tape, before launching into a headlock with Sands.

'Get off me you crazy bastard,' Sands wails, clambering in beside Cigar.

'Stop the fuck-actin', ing,' Mad-dog yells, looking in his large rear-view mirror. Next comes The Weasel, real name

Brian Fanning, another one of the dynasty. He carries a T-Square in his left hand but mysteriously no schoolbag. Farrell does not escape a sharp poke of the end in the ribs. The Weasel is only a Fourth Year, but seems permitted to the back seat hierarchy, slotting to the far right, inside Crazy. Finally, Marcus, The Daddy. He is not as muscular as Cigar but his face tells of someone who could kill.

I see Freddy take up a seat across the aisle next to O'Brien but it is time to stop looking around me as The Daddy is looking around him. The bus is hardly moving before my ponytail is tugged. The usual pattern is light tugs, gradually becoming more vicious, until the hair feels like it will fall out. When I sit low in the seat, seeking the safety of the backrest, a hand comes down with force on the top of my head.

'It's a hard station you're in, Brush,' Farrell says sympathetically.

Art becomes interesting. I enjoy an absurd camaraderie with Bendy. I now believe him to have an unhealthy appreciation of the odours of Tipex and other adhesives, which might explain his excessive laughter at my every utterance. I invent a brand of sugar energy drink and design a graphic marketing campaign. I am quite proud of my innovation 'Fizzer,' which I imagine will be a mixture of milk and lemonade. Mr Kirk says he is not sure how it will taste but does praise my conceptual drawings.

German is not that difficult. I can now count to ten. I try to move my chair slightly nearer to Alannah. I spend most of the class attempting to bang my elbow into hers. At one stage she looks over. I pretend not to notice.

The classes with Mr Fogarty are a joke. No one listens to him. One morning, Rebecca asks him how much vegetables are in supermarkets with blue eyes wide open and biro between teeth. He spends the whole class estimating the price of a pound of tomatoes and other items.

Quirke, Farrell and O'Brien write quickly, getting much of their homework done. This is a great idea, I decide. I get quite a good bit written up while Mr Fogarty tells the beautiful Rebecca about the current prices of iceberg lettuce.

I am amazed at how neatly O'Brien can write. I remember showing him how to make small Ks in first class. Actually, I showed most of them. Dad had started teaching me the alphabet before I ever started school. I could read very well by the age of six.

'Thank you so much for your help,' Rebecca smiles as the bell goes. Mr Fogarty nods politely and walks out of room ten with his extremely old-fashioned bag.

'He is such an ass,' Rebecca says to Orla. There is something I do not like about this, but I still think Rebecca is very nice indeed. Maybe Mr Fogarty should retire.

By the third week, there are a number of issues which irk me. Martin Ainsworth slyly attacks every time we meet on the corridor.

'Challenge him, Brush,' Quirke says, noticing one of the fair-haired one's covert attacks.

'He's all piss and wind,' Farrell adds.

'Give him a good fucking belt,' O'Brien concludes.

Mann persists in digging me in the ribs when he and his crew arrive at the prefab door during breaks. There is a similar problem with Carvey and then there is the perennial mystery of the ponytail-puller stroke head-whacker on the yellow bus. On the bright side, I believe I am making good progress with Alannah's elbow and I may even soon speak with Rebecca.

Mr Fogarty is not in and we have a substitute who persists in attempting to involve the class in a discussion about Irish society, through Irish. Few people in the class speak Irish and less are interested in the discussion, so there is not much participation, but it is not possible to get any homework done.

As I take out my books at seven that evening, I realise I will be working all night. I have had a long journey home with some cunt pulling my ponytail and Martin Ainsworth today resumed groin-centred attacks which may have already sterilised me. I want a mug of sugary tea after dinner, but the electric kettle is broken and there is no time to wait for the one on the range to boil.

I look at the list in the diary. Mrs Morahan loved my story about the bus and wants more. However, she has given us mostly extremely boring assignments since, including verb searching and the appalling letter-writing exercises. Tonight we are asked to develop the Wordsworth line 'I wandered lonely as a cloud' into a poem of our own. Lonely, lonely as a cloud. Despite this being an exciting prospect normally, this evening, I don't know, I just can't do it. I stare at a blank page for some time, scratching my head. I put the English copy away and take up my maths book. Mean, median, mode and range, mean, median, mode and range.

Now there are some distractions. Dad wants to play the guitar, Mam is on the phone, my brother and sister are yelling out in the living room, watching TV. I resort to my bedroom. I want Doyle to call to give me an excuse to take a break but he never comes when he is wanted.

On the bed, I try to arrange my homework. Geography – irrigation, soils and percolations. The art work is taking up a lot of room in my 'Jack's Army' schoolbag. Mr Kirk has asked me to arrange my current drawings in the right order. I try to see what paintings I can leave at home. I find my Fizzer poster paint had not dried fully and had stuck onto another sketch I had started in the last class. I pull at the sheets and the Fizzer poster tears in half. A lump of dried paint bursts open and from within liquid oozes out all over my geography copy. Mrs Sharpe will not like that. It's half seven now and I've nothing done! I cry, I burst into tears! I tear the Fizzer poster into bits, I throw the maths book against the wall, I hurl the geography copy, dripping with paint, at the wardrobe. I lie on the bed, pull the blanket over and close my eyes.

We are in Room Ten at lunchtime. Melvin sits behind me, talking to Conway about tractors. Quirke wraps up his lunch.

'We go for a walk,' he says. I get up with Farrell and O'Brien. 'Melvin?'

'…they made a new model,' Melvin is saying, sitting back in his chair. 'Nah, I'm waiting here with T.'

We walk out into the light. Crazy is running with a football. He kicks it at Sands' groin.

'You muppet, Crazy,' Sands shouts in his smooth English accent, as he makes a protective cross with his arms. The ball bounces off them and rolls on the ground.

'What did you call me?' Crazy roars, launching onto Sands. Everyone knows it's light-hearted, as they wrestle awkwardly.

'Will ye calm down?' Cigar says, picking the ball up and shaking his head.

'Idiots,' Quirke says quietly. 'Come on, we'll go down the trees.'

'Isn't that where the smokers are?' I say.

'Ah, Brush,' Farrell says, with that irritatingly superior tone.

'Is it not a bit risky?' I look to O'Brien, who just stares ahead.

The teacher on yard duty is looking through a folder near the prefab entrance and we soon move out of sight. We walk down the winding track into the trees. I can feel my heart beating.

'Does Pete come down here much?'

'Don't worry Brush, you're not smoking,' Quirke says.

'Yes, but will he know that?'

'Pete's down the town having a steak dinner,' Farrell says, assertively.

Small clusters of blue emerge. A pale Second Year looks up around the leaves.

'Down by the wall. There's too many in the grass already. '

'We're not smoking though,' I say, but no one seems to hear me.

'There's Needham behind that tree,' Quirke says.

Needham is nodding, talking to Carvey, as we walk up to them. He looks around sharply at the sound of footsteps.

'Jesus! Don't be creeping up on us like that,' Needham says.

'What's the craic?' Quirke says.

Carvey holds his fag butt with a practised ease, hooking the red-hot end toward his palm. He sucks on it hungrily. A thin stream of smoke drifts from his half-clenched fist.

'Are you playing for Davitts on Sunday, Carvey?' Farrell says. Carvey nods carelessly.

'Under 16?' Quirke says.

'Fair play,' Farrell says.

'Don't give a fuck really,' Carvey says. He drops the butt on the ground, pushing it flat.

'Carvey, you're meant to put that in your pockets,' Needham says, with surprising concern.

'That's one for Mac to sweep up,' Carvey says. 'Give us another, we have time.'

'Aright, if you're sure,' Needham says, looking around, unzipping his fly and feeling around for a moment, before producing a crumpled box of Carrolls. He tosses a cigarette to Carvey.

'It's not infected, no?' Carvey says as he lights up, with a seductive spin of a lighter. Needham has made the Carrolls box disappear quicker than Paul Daniels.

I notice a few other groups of smokers crouched along the high wall at the end of the trees. Some are less careful; standing brazenly in front of the inner lines of greenery.

'We should probably go, it's a bit risky, huh?' I say to O'Brien.

Now there is an odd hush. 'Pete!' the shout comes and suddenly everyone is running. I hurry around in a circle not knowing where I am going.

'Getting out of me fucking way,' Needham yells, pushing past me, as everyone tries to scale the high wall. I climb up, my chin hits the ledge at the top and I slide miserably back to the ground. I see Carvey and Needham leap athletically over, not handicapped, it seems by their smoker's cough. Farrell and Quirke are long gone. O'Brien's butterarse disappears through a hedge. I follow him.

'You there!' the deep voice booms. I look around and Peter F. Shylock, his face a darker purple than usual, walks quickly up.

'My office. Now.'

The pit of my stomach erupts. 'But, sir–'

'Now.' Peter F. Shylock pounds past, in the direction of O'Brien.

I walk back up the winding track, feeling as though my life is over. Nothing matters. I am on my way to the office now and unknown punishments for merely standing near a couple of smokers. There is no smell of tobacco on me but I cannot see Peter F. Shylock sniffing my shirt.

Sands and Crazy are still pushing each other around the court. The Daddy sits on a small battered chair in the corner of the tennis courts, with Cigar and a few other Leaving Certs. I see The Weasel puffing on a cigarette at the wire door, carefully watching the trees for Peter F. Shylock, the glow within his fingers brightening every time he drags.

I am somewhat relieved to find others also waiting at the bottom of the stairs, at the radiator adjacent to The Principal's office.

Mann stands with his arms folded, his hips gyrating slightly as though to some invisible beat. Beside him, Houston leans against the radiator, eyes closed, while Corless, at the stairs handrail, examines something he has just plucked from his ear.

'Brush, where are you going?' Mann says, as I stand awkwardly near them. 'You don't even smoke!'

'Mann, will you quieten down, I'm trying to sleep,' Houston complains.

'I was down at the woods with Farrell and them. They were all on the wall, I couldn't get out in time,' I say.

'Whatever you do, don't squeal,' Mann says. 'We were at the back of the complex when Pete came. He–,'

At that moment, Peter F. Shylock's silhouette fills the top of the stairs. 'Hands out of the pockets before I get down there, Mann,' he growls.

The Principal slowly descends the steps and walks up really close to us as we stand taut, like telegraph poles. Even Houston looks remarkably awake. Amazingly, Peter F. Shylock does appear to be sniffing us, his nose is no more than an inch from my face as he slowly walks along.

'You,' he says to me, as he stands at the office door. 'Keep away from the woods. They're out of bounds. Now get back to your classroom. You three – inside.'

I gratefully hurry away, leaving the others to their fate. My slate is still clean, and I will not be chancing the woods again.

Every day, Quirke, Farrell and O'Brien get much of their homework done in Mr Fogarty's class. I try to keep up, but I am losing interest, there are too many subjects, my head is full of Rebecca and Alannah, avoiding Martin Ainsworth, Carvey, Mann, the sadist on the yellow bus. I spend most breaks now at the prefab doors watching for the nipple stroke testicle freak.

Carvey slaps me across the head as he passes in the corridor. 'That ponytail. I don't like it. It's coming off one of these days,' he says.

When Mann digs me in the ribs, I stare threateningly, but he just laughs. 'Give him a belt back,' Quirke advises later, at lunch in room ten.

'He's a big cunt,' I say.

'Full of shit,' Farrell adds. 'Give him a fucking box.'

Even after the Keadin-Melvin debacle, there is still a hunger amongst the First Year community for scraps.

'Would you take on one of the room eight skins?' Quirke says to me.

I pretend I didn't hear him. To beat someone in a scrap though, or even lose gallantly, witnessed by half the school, would probably stop the jabbing of Mann and Carvey.

But scrapping is a risky business. Two Fourth Years get into an argument over a bag of crisps and the scrap is set for a Friday at last break. Crowds hurry down to the prefab cloakroom. It is impossible to see anything. Everyone just runs around indiscriminately. Somewhere amongst the morass of bodies, the two scrappers are said to be engaging. There is a roar and the familiar scream of 'Pete!' I wait at the door as long as I dare, as others hurry away. I find myself fascinated with this atmosphere, the sense of aggression, of uncertainty, of danger.

One of the scrappers' nose is bleeding, the other has a cut over his eyes. They hurry out past me, their associates following behind. Ryan is somehow involved, he dashes into the corridor, carrying a sheet of paper, a pencil professionally nestled behind his ear.

'I'm calling it a draw, Kev,' he whispers. But Peter F. Shylock is later reported to have caught up with the pair of fighters, and suspended them for three weeks.

'How did you get on with the geography for Sharpe?' Farrell asks me during Mr Fogarty's class one day. Mr Fogarty is attempting to halt a wrestling match near the window by speedily waving his biro.

'I haven't done it yet,' I say. I am working on a Liverpool F.C. crest on my homework diary cover.

'She never checks it anyway, too busy eating the head of someone,' I add. Farrell turns over to O'Brien.

'Did you do that irrigation question?'

'I did yeah, it's handy enough…'

I turn around to Melvin. 'Are you doing them maths?'

'Did some of them,' Melvin looks up.

'Sure O'Leary doesn't give a fuck if you do them or not,' Conway puts in.

'No, he's sound,' Melvin agrees.

'Do you have a highlighter I could borrow?' Rebecca looks at me, her blue eyes reflecting the fluorescent light.

'No,' I confirm with a more officious tone than I intended.

'Oh,' Rebecca says.

As we get on the bus that evening, I am standing right behind her. I can smell her perfume, her hair. She has a pink and white school bag. She turns around.

'Call me tonight,' she says.

'I don't have your number,' I blurt.

'It's in the book,' Rebecca says, as she sits in one of the seats near the top.

Mr Kirk tries to explain objectivity one freezing morning, when he finally manages to pull himself away from his precious three boxes. The prefab glass shakes against the late October winds.

'You need to be able to stand back from the items you draw, aesthetically speaking. This bowl of oranges,' Mr Kirk says, nodding at the bowl on his desk. 'You need to see it all, not just one dimension, do you understand children? You boy...' I am looking at the ceiling thinking about something. I realise Mr Kirk is looking at me. 'Stop doing that.'

There is a twitter. I look around. What? As we leave, the girl that claimed we were a couple the first week, Aine Muldoon, who has turned out to be a pretty if overtly stout, black-haired girl, comes near me in the prefab corridor. Two other giggling girls link each side of her.

'Hey Brush, did you have a good pick?' Aine says, before bursting into laughter, accompanied by her friends. They hurry past me. I realise they were watching me picking my nose throughout Mr Kirk's class.

After Hallowe'en, the school year moves towards darkness, cold mornings, heavy wind and rain. I have dispensed with my beret now. My 'Jack's Army' schoolbag has lost the sprightly clean look it had in the sunlight of September. There is a constant threat on my ponytail. Needham keeps saying things like 'We'll have the scissor in next week for ya, Brush.'

'Don't worry Brush. They won't go near you,' Farrell assures me.

I spend most evenings talking to Doyle about TV programmes, his antics in sixth class and my frustration with First Year.

'The amount of work we get down there is crazy,' I tell him. Not that I do it all. I do what will be checked. I am more than disappointed to learn that room eight's English teacher, Mr Smith, instructs the class to create their own weekly newspapers. Mrs Morahan is focussing on poetry which bores me. I think about these things sometimes on the way home on the bus, as the rain beats against the windows, after the threat of ponytail pulling has waned.

The German class was fun the first week as we had a quiz and that allowed for me to answer one or two questions and let Alannah to hear my voice and perhaps look at me while I was speaking. However, since then it has become very boring, concentrating on learning the language and culture of Germany. One day we are asked to say our favourite bands in German. I choose *Bon Jovi* and *Jive Bunny* and spend the class lettering *Bon Jovi* on the cover of my German book.

A girl from the class later tells me everyone sniggered when I said I liked *Jive Bunny*.

'They're not even a real band, they just join other songs together,' she says dismissively.

We are standing in the tennis courts at lunchtime, I, Farrell and Quirke. O'Brien is finishing off maths homework in room ten.

Melvin and Conway are also there, the last I heard they were discussing winter dosage techniques on weanlings.

Needham and Carvey come through the wire doorway, followed by Mann, Corless and Houston.

'Come on Brush, it's time for a haircut,' Needham says, pulling a large silver scissors from his pocket. He comes up close to me. I notice some room eights arriving, Ryan, the fat man Keadin, with Keegan and the tiny Murphy bringing up the rear.

'Fuck off,' I say simply.

'Come on lads, grab him,' Needham says, snapping the scissors together in the afternoon air.

'Leave it,' I say, my hand shaking a little. The tall boys crowd around me.

They push closer. They seem to wait for someone to grab me. I back to the wire fence. Farrell and Quirke have edged away.

'Off, off, off!' A few of them shout. I notice Ryan in particular. Murphy dances on the edge of the group. I envy his smallness now, too tiny to even be a target.

'Come on,' Needham says, with a friendly tone. 'You'll look a lot better for the girls,' he continues, with a wise tone. The thought of Alannah in the same minute as Needham is absurd.

'Gerry, a chair please,' Needham shouts to Carvey.

The Daddy's chair is conveniently not in use and it is flung in amongst the bodies, the throne of respect now to be the amateur barber's chair of shame for me.

'Off, off, off!' the chant continues.

'Sit down there, good lad,' Keadin says. Needham takes me by the shoulders, I knew he'd make the move, now I struggle to escape, Carvey locks onto my waist, Keadin, with his muscles wobbling, pulls one leg, Keegan, looking nonplussed and mysteriously licking his lips, grabs the other and I am airborne.

My rear is flung to the seat of the chair and I feel Needham flicking at my ponytail.

I hear the scissors snap and I try to get off but there are many hands on me and I cannot move, it is like I am nailed down.

'Off, off, off!'

'Bastards,' I mutter through clenched teeth.

Needham pushes my neck forward, I feel someone grab my ponytail.

'That's my seat,' I hear a voice. There is a hush and one last snap of Needham's scissors. The curls of my ponytail still rest on my neck.

The crowd step back. Standing a few feet away are The Weasel, Cigar and in the middle, Marcus The Daddy.

'What are ye girls doing with my seat?'

'Nawthing Dad, just having a bit of craic. This fella needs a haircut, see,' Needham says shakily.

'Oh he does, does he?' The Daddy booms.

Marcus walks up through the group which has thinned out, eyes focussed now on the Leaving Certs, trying to assess their consensus.

'Why do you say that?' Maurice looks at me and then Needham.

'It's to do with–,' Carvey starts.

'Shut it.' Carvey looks to the ground. Maurice is a good foot over Carvey.

'We reckoned – we reckoned the ponytail wan't part of the uniform, see,' Needham wobbles out.

'No I don't see,' Maurice says. 'Are you working for Sharp-tits, now is that it?'

Needham fiddles with the scissors. 'No, I–,'

'You her nancy-boy, is that it?'

'I...I,'

The other First Years have edged across the courts. No one wants to be implicated by The Daddy in this mood, it seems.

'You!' Maurice looks at me. 'Out of my fucking seat. Don't let me see you there again.'

I nod and hurry over to the wire fence. 'There's a new lunch menu in the school, Dad,' The Weasel says. It is the first time I have heard him speak, his voice is light, almost girlish, but with a stinging undercurrent that is snake-like. The Weasel gathers a fistful of loose gravel from the ground. 'Maybe Sharp-tits' nancy-boy will test it out.'

'Yeah, maybe,' Maurice nods, happily. 'Sit down there now,' he says to Needham, helping him into the chair. Needham conforms to The Daddy's guiding hands. The Daddy looks at The Weasel's handful of gravel, takes up a pinch, sniffs it.

'Not bad. You know,' Maurice says, looking at Needham. 'People say stones, like, stones're not nice. They're awful liars. Trying to keep them for themselves, you see. But I reckon they're lovely, well, we both do, don't we, Brian? '

'We do,' nods The Weasel.

'When you get used of them, they're like…they're tasty, do you know?' Marcus says warmly. Needham nods.

'You'll try a few, will yeah?'

Needham smiles. 'Will ya!' Marcus shouts.

'I will, I will!' Needham says, enthusiastically nodding. Marcus holds out the gravel in his hand.

'Go on, don't be afraid. There's plenty more, isn't there, Brian?'

'There is,' The Weasel confirms.

Needham nods and takes a pinch. He puts the little stones into his mouth. Some stick to his lips. 'Nice aren't they?' Marcus says. Needham nods, his lips moving slowly.

'People are awful liars, Dad,' The Weasel says.

'Awful liars, Brian,' Marcus says.

Now the bus is a more pleasant place to travel in. My ponytail is rarely pulled any more. It is, indeed, an endless advantage to have been favoured by The Daddy. Even Freddy Fanning says hello to me in the evenings.

He usually sits a seat back across the aisle, beside O'Brien with his face toward the back row.

'No one tried to cut the hair today, Brush?' he says one evening.

'No.'

'The brother sorted that for ya.'

'He did.'

'We look after our own here. Pure wanker that Needham. His brothers are too.' Quirke had told us Needham has many older brothers, all now finished school. Perhaps they had been Daddies at one stage.

I am not learning much German, though I have not yet missed a class. I nudge Alannah's desk one day, her biro rolls off onto the ground. I pick it up, looking at her as I leave it on her desk.

'Thanks a million,' she smiles.

I grunt and return to my copy as though intent on serious scholarship. Apart from that, progress with getting to speak to her has been generally slow.

Mann has persisted with digging me in the ribs every time he passes. I push him away one day. It is a weak attempt, hardly stirring him, my hands seem to sink into his flab.

'What are you at, you cunt?' Mann says, pushing me back hard. He seems even more insurmountable to me. 'Cut yer fucking hair.'

I glare at him. When he is gone, Farrell again berates me.

'You wanta give that wanker a belt on the nose. Will you scrap him? Quirke will set it up. For the end of term, what do you say, Brush? Gives you a week or two to prepare.'

'I–'

'Go on, he won't leave you alone until you do. You could take him, I'd say,' Farrell presses.

'You could,' O'Brien adds.

'Definitely,' Quirke concludes.

On the way home that evening I think about a scrap with Mann. Mann is taller than me and heavier. I've never really had a fight before, apart from O'Brien busting my nose in third class. I did manage to wind him in the stomach that time, but since then I'd managed to avoid them. Now, there did not seem to be a way out. It would be better to scrap Mann and get hammered. At least then I would have faced him down. The avoiding the issue was worse, it was prolonging the torture.

I never called Rebecca, wouldn't be able to do that, but I continue to admire her from the desk behind in room ten. We move the seats around for the Christmas Exams. I try to manoeuvre mine up toward Rebecca's seat, not that I want to cog, just so I could be a bit nearer her and smell her hair.

'What are you doing, Brush?' she says as she notices. 'Don't be picking your nose near me.'

'I don't pick my nose.' I feel heat on my skin.

'You do, you pick your nose,' Rebecca confirms, closing up her text book. 'You were seen.'

The Sale of Work was held every December, according to Quirke. Stands are set up in the assembly hall. We take a look over the lunch break on the Wednesday before. A prefect soon ushers us out to the entrance porch. Farrell lounges at the entrance doors, while Quirke and O'Brien lean against the school notice board.

'Pete's gone for lunch,' Farrell says. 'Happy days for the smokers.'

Peter F. Shylock goes to lunch every day. He leaves at various times, keeping the smokers' spies guessing, but this tactic is devalued somewhat by his habit of parking his Ford

Granada right at the entrance. Mac, acting principal in Peter F. Shylock's absence usually spends the lunch hour leafing through his precious blue folder outside the prefabs.

'You could take on Mann down at the Sale of Work,' Quirke says.

'Yeah, sure, you could do it down the town, no need to be arsin' around up here watching for Pete,' Farrell says, with some excitement.

'Be a bit risky though. Guards might come,' Quirke says, pensively.

'Fuck that,' I put in.

I still have not actually agreed to fight Mann, although it is now relayed to me that Mann thinks I want to scrap him and he and his crew of Corless and Houston give me a wide berth. They no longer come across the yard to talk to us at the door to the prefab and when they see us passing room nine, they ignore us. Needham and Carvey provide the conduit of communication.

'He reckons he's going to kill ya,' Needham says on Friday. 'He says you're a fucking queer with a girl's haircut.'

Carvey has stopped hitting me in the ribs, perhaps waiting to see how the Mann scrap turns out. Needham too, seems more amicable after his stone-tasting ceremony.

'Go for the nose, that's my advice,' Needham says.

'Mann is just a bag of wind,' Carvey comments carelessly, as they shiver near the complex in the freezing breeze. But I know they are hardly on my side, they will be reporting back to their room nine colleague with any information.

'What's your best hand?' Needham says.

'Either,' I say, carefully.

'He's a ciotog, see him playing volleyball,' Carvey says.

'If he gets you in a headlock, you're fucked,' Needham warns.

'He'll be aright, The Brush'll whack him,' Farrell intervenes.

Mam drives me and Melvin down to the Sale of Work the following Sunday.

'I wonder will Mann be there,' I say, turning around to Melvin.

'Why, are you scrapping him?' Melvin says.

'I don't want to, they organised it.'

'Tell them you don't know him, that's what I always say.'

'Yeah, but I do know him, don't I? That was alright for you after the first week or so, but now?'

'Sure, they'd want you fighting every week. It's alright for them watching it. Tell them you don't know them,' Melvin concludes.

'Yeah but–,'

'If you could stop here,' Melvin says to mam.

'Howya T,' Melvin says, as Conway gets in the back beside him.

They immediately launch into a specialised discussion of winter foodstuffs for beef cattle. Mam drops us at the end of the avenue, where Farrell and Quirke stand.

'Mann is up there at the assembly hall with Houston, Corless and a few other fuckers from room nine,' Farrell says. 'Needham and Carvey were here a while ago, but you couldn't trust them pricks. They reckon he has a few of the village tools with him as well. You wouldn't know what would happen so you better stick with us, alright Brush?'

As we walk over the speed bumps Mad-dog bounces over every morning, it seems like we might be ambushed at any moment. I look around nervously.

'Oh. Here's trouble,' Farrell says. I follow his gaze and am surprisingly relieved to see Marley and O'Toole emerge from the grass behind the trees.

'How's the hards?' Marley says grinning. He carries a small empty plastic bag with him.

'Going shopping, Johnny?' Farrell says.

'Sort a.'

'Hear there's a bit of hassle in the pipes,' O'Toole says.

'No hassle, you're alright,' O'Brien says, quickly.

'I know I'm alright,' O'Toole snaps. He pulls something from his pocket, flicking it. The blade glints in the December light.

'Any hassle, sure give us a shout. We don't like Mann either.'

'No. Fat cunt,' Marley adds.

'We won't be calling on them,' Farrell says, when they are gone.

'Very dodgy. See the blade?' O'Brien says. I tire of this adulation of shitheads.

'That's all for show,' I say, dismissively. 'He wouldn't know how to use it.'

'Do you reckon, Brush?' Farrell says, with some derision. 'You know the father was put away for stabbing someone. I'd say he taught yer man a few tricks before he went off, don't you?'

Farrell's words ring in my ears like Mrs Sharpe's, as we resume the walk to the school. Cut it off.

As we near the entrance porch, I am more fearful of running away from Mann than the pain he might inflict on me. The worst thing would be to desert the challenge, but it is not something I have ruled out.

A poster is extended across the stage in the assembly hall, announcing the event. Cheerful looking woman walk through the crowds holding tickets. There are trays of cakes, buns, and pastries spread out on some tables with junk on others; radios, battery chargers, sets of spanners with some, the most useful, common sizes, missing. Christmas music plays in the background. Other stalls sell magazines, ornaments, cheap plastic jewellery. Peter F. Shylock is nowhere to be seen, nor Mac. The only teacher I find is the obscure French woman, whose name nobody can pronounce.

There is no sign of Mann, Carvey or indeed any other students, apart from a few bored looking prefects.

'What the fuck, load of shite,' Conway diagnoses.

'That Needham is an awful bullshitter,' Quirke says.

We spend the day playing pool in a pub down the town. Marley and O'Toole pass through, their plastic bag is full.

'How'd the scrap go?' Marley says, but he doesn't wait for an answer.

'Ye didn't actually go up to that old crap,' Needham says from the door of room nine. I stand at our door, peeking up the corridor on lookout, as we wait for Mrs Morahan. Farrell and O'Brien are playfully wrestling within, in the centre of some desks. 'Sure tis just the swots and prefects that go to that. A few stale buns.'

'I thought you were going,' I say, tiring of Needham's voice. Needham comes up the corridor quickly.

'Mann says he'll scrap ya last break Friday before the holidays,' Needham says in a low tone. 'If ye get caught then ye can't be suspended. Pete thinks all the scraps now are organised for the prefab cloakroom. We'll have it at the back of the tennis courts. No one will suspect that.'

'The new heavyweight champion,' Farrell roars from behind, his arms around O'Brien's waist.

'What is going on here?' Mrs Morahan says from behind me. 'Why are you out in the hall?

'Go straight for the nose,' Quirke says as we sit in room ten during lunch hour on Friday.

'Yeah. Think about nothing but his fuckin' nose,' says Farrell.

'You could break it,' O'Brien warns.

'Don't know what bones he has, don't think he has any,' Farrell puts in.

'Like yer man, you know Pack Dolan,' Melvin says, laughing to Conway.

71

'Oh yeah. He's good on the hopper isn't he?' Conway says.

'Did he cut yer turf?'

'Oh he did, yeah. He…'

I look back at the door. I do not want to fight Mann. I doubt I will get near his nose. He will probably break my jaw and who knows what else. He is taller than me and heavier than me. What am I to do?

Shortly after the bell at 2.45pm, we hurry down the corridor. Everything must happen fast, the last break is just ten minutes. I am wishing it was over and we were running back up. That is, if I am still able to run by then.

'I'm not fighting him,' I say to Quirke at the end of the corridor, but he doesn't hear me or he ignores me. Farrell and O'Brien hurry me along.

A crowd have gathered at the back of the tennis courts. Ryan is in the centre, holding his fist underneath his chin in the guise of a microphone and appears to be conducting pre-fight interviews.

Murphy stands next to him holding a piece of paper and a pen.

'We'll give ye evens on The Panzer and two-to-one on The Brush, lads. Ten p could make ye a pound,' he says. One of the potential pundits frown at this mathematical equation.

Keadin leans against the wire fence, adopting the expression of someone who has somehow managed to avoid the day of judgement, at least for now.

'Brush, Brush, Brush!' Carvey and Needham are shouting. I am absurdly disappointed that Mann's own roommates seem to have betrayed him.

Now, I see Mann. Houston, awake for once, is whispering something to my opponent who stands still, like a placid balloon.

I decide what to do. I put my head down and before Ryan can make some kind of introduction, I simply run at Mann. My head connects with Mann's stomach and we career around in a circle before a group of shouting bodies clamber over us. A fist connects with my nose and blood spills out. I am lying on the ground, everyone is running.

Murphy stands beside me. 'Come on Brush, get the fuck out of here, Pete's coming.'

Clutching my nose, I hurry out of the tennis courts, following the crowds into the prefab. Murphy hands me a tissue from the jacks.

'Thanks,' I say, leaving him at room eight. He's sound, Murphy.

As Mad-dog swerves around the bends, worryingly more concerned with the animals in the fields than the road in front of him, I look forward to the Christmas holidays. Three weeks away from dark mornings, eight classes per day, the ball-grabbing Martin Ainsworth, the mysterious ponytail fanatic who, although he had taken something of a hiatus in mid-term, had reactivated activities in the past few weeks. Often now the skull slap was preferred to the ponytail pull.

I am still no nearer to identifying him. There is never a hint on anyone's face when I look around. No one offers any clues. It will be a relief too, not to have to worry anymore about fighting Mann. It seems my head butt charge and subsequent nose busting has announced myself as a 'Man' in First Year.

Carvey has stopped jabbing me in the ribs, for the most part. I still received the odd shoulder charge, but I take that as more of a brotherly bonding exercise than outright intimidation. So moving out of the first term, things are not that bleak.

During the holidays, I find myself making Christmas Specials of the newspapers I had been making in sixth class last year, it is the end of a decade and I produce an extensive thirty-two page review of the past ten years.

I go out some nights with dad to the fields in the moonlight, checking on pregnant ewes. It's cold, and I'd rather be inside watching The James Whale Radio Show. Sometimes I have to hold the ewe while Dad pulls a lamb. I don't like to see the pain the sheep does be in during labour. It's great when the lambs turn out alright, but sometimes they are stillborn and we have to bury them outside the sheep shed. The new lambs get beastings from the mother soon as they're out. We use a long tube attached to a kind of syringe. I'm always afraid I'll choke it, you have to push the tube down its throat, but it really brightens when the milk gets to its stomach.

I become preoccupied with one lamb dad puts in the shed near the house. The ewe died during birth. I have to feed him with Frisky every day. Frisky is a kind of a powdered milk, and when I was younger, I used to eat it by the teaspoon. It's lovely stuff. I still take a pinch of it when making up the bottle for the lamb. Morning and evening the little fella gets his feed. I start doing this the first week I am off and even by January he has grown so much, it's amazing. His body is warm and pulsing as he sucks down the milk mixture. He's a ram, so he hasn't got a great future ahead. First, he'll be castrated and his tail will be cut off. Admittedly, with the somewhat more humane chemical rings which slowly burn the flesh. An improvement on granda's method, the knife cutting the tail off and slicing open the sac, where he would tear the testicles out with his teeth. Then when the lamb is fat enough, he'll be off to see the butcher.

I enjoy the routine of feeding him. The rest of the day I lounge around the house, sometimes helping dad with fencing, feeding cattle. I don't go near any school work. I prefer to make Christmas newspapers, comics, magazines. I write a radio play. I record it with my sister and we play it on Christmas Day after dinner. It's a kind of a morbid existentialist thing. My grandparents look confused.

We spend New Year's Eve in front of the telly, watching old politicians talk about the country's chances in the futuristic world we are moving into. The immediate future for me is the impending arrival of my Christmas Report in the first week of January.

Mam and Dad are in shock. I fail four subjects. Art, German, Geography and History. I do get a B in English. I try to concentrate on the good results.

I am not doing enough homework is the parental consensus. Actually, I am hardly doing any as I look back over the previous three months. I did pass more than half of the subjects. Still, a career in journalism will be difficult with these scores.

These are only the Christmas tests, I conclude and not that essentially important. I begin a new comic called The Deano.

The morning of January eleventh is dark, wet and very windy. I am blown in the door of Mad-dog's bus. He insists on seeing the new term's ticket immediately. By the time Assembly arrives, I have still not fully woken up. Eleven was the earliest I arose in the past weeks.

'Smoking is completely prohibited,' Peter F. Shylock is saying. I do make a conscious effort to improve my grades. I try to see what I am missing in the history class. Mac goes into intricate details about early settlers. I discover the primitive villages were actually around where we live now, just thousands of years ago. They used bronze and stone tools to chop wood, ate grass and lived in houses made of dried cow shit apparently.

Mr Kirk was a bollocks to fail me. He said to me my work was good and then he fails me. I draw a big clock when we are told to paint something related to time. He hums and haws at it.

'That's good,' Ryan confirms, as he glances over, after Mr Kirk has gone back to his three boxes. I am careful now with the giggling audience across the room. One day, Aine comes over and kisses me on the cheek.

'It's for a bet, sorry,' she says, as she walks back to her seat. My nose fetish seems to have been forgiven and my stomach seems to lighten a bit. Her lips felt warm on my cheek. Bendy guffaws and he hasn't even opened today's glue yet.

'I think Aine has a thing for ya,' Ryan says, pulling on a fag near the complex door one morning.

'Fuck that, she's an awful dog,' I say, looking around for Peter F. Shylock. Ryan can be incredibly stupid, not even the Leaving Certs smoke this near the school.

'Ah, still,' Ryan says. 'A fanny's a fanny.'

Quirke, Farrell and O Brien move into overdrive in Fogarty's class. I am starting to think they are machines. They take out their homework religiously when Fogarty comes in and after thirty five minutes, they have pages and pages neatly written out. Not everyone takes advantage. Melvin and Conway discuss spring lambs in detail. Orla and Rebecca continue to ask Mr Fogarty ridiculous questions, which he bizarrely attempts to answer. He tries to teach Irish, but few pay any heed. I start inscribing an LFC crest on my desk. There is no way I can do homework in that class. It's like being at the mart with dad.

I enjoy P.E. Miss Tuohy is much more enthusiastic about teaching sport then she is about teaching French. She bounds around the complex floor, explaining special warm-up exercises. She talks to us about the Irish soccer team, instructs on badminton and volleyball. I am not good at Volleyball. I can't seem to get the slamming action quite right. But usually, we play indoor soccer. I am not bad. My team of Farrell, Quirke, O'Brien and Melvin gets to the final of a mini-tournament, but we lose to Carvey's team. Jimmy Moran is a wonderful player and dominates everything. Joseph is reputed to be even better, but he refuses to play at all, sitting on a bench at the wall, in his P.E. gear, arms folded, stonily staring into the middle distance. Jimmy scores a hat-trick in the final and coughs his smoker's guts out at the end as Miss Tuohy congratulates him.

I play badminton another day with Keadin. It's the only sport he can play because he doesn't have to move off the one spot. I expect to win quite easily. But when he starts serving, he beats the shuttle a mile up into the air and with the light coming through the Perspex in the roof, I can't see it coming down. He keeps winning the serve because he keeps winning the point. Consequently he beats me 10-nil. Imagine been beaten 10-nil by Keadin. I am disgusted.

'You don't use that formula for Question 17,' Farrell says at the complex, the first week of February.

'Do you not?' O' Brien says.

'No, they're only for the ones on Page 29,' Quirke confirms.

I get bored and walk around the yard. Sands is throwing apple cores at Crazy. Cigar is laughing in the corner. The Weasel and The Daddy are sitting on two stools smoking, the fag ends glowing within the curled fingers. In a few months, they will be free of here, while we will have four more years. The time stretches out before me like a bottomless pit.

I walk up along the wire fence, down the winding track, to the first cluster of trees. Murphy, still only four foot I estimate, swings on the lower branches. There is no sign of his associates from room eight.

'Howya Brush,' he says. He is collecting conkers. He has a pile at the base of one trunk. I look through them.

'Did you ever roast them?' I say, thinking of a Dickens story or something.

'Roast them? Can you roast them?' he says. Something I saw in a nature book comes back to me.

'Yeah look, you open them.' I break open the shell, releasing the shiny brown chestnut within. Murphy is excited.

'How do you roast them?' Murphy says.

'I–I think you put them in a pot and cook them,' I say, vaguely.

We start to go down the village on Friday nights. Melvin calls for me on his bike. We usually go to the shop before it closes at ten. I buy Chickatees, a small bottle of Coca-Cola and a stick of Bubble King.

We meet Doyle at the school yard, across from his house. We have a game of three-goals-in in the car park. Doyle is not much good. Melvin is like a tank and impossible to tackle. I feel I have some skill. I try to be like Maradona, dribbling, swerving, feinting and volleying. There is a great buzz after. Melvin has an awful hard shot. The wall zaps when he shoots. One night he misses the wall and the ball flies over the wall and smashes the school window. The staff room window.

We cycle home as fast as we can. We give the village school a wide berth for a few weeks.

'There was a big inquiry,' Doyle reports later.

One day when I'm up at the trees talking to Murphy who is clambering between braches, Mann comes along.

'Did you see Corless anywhere?' he asks us.

'No?'

'What are ye at there?' Mann says. I feel protective, like this is an intimate thing between me and Murphy and no other bastard is allowed to get involved.

'Nothing. Picking conkers,' Murphy says.

'Oh yeah. You can roast them,' Mann says, much to my surprise.

'We know,' Murphy nods, as if it was him that told me.

'Mann, what are you at?' Corless says, coming around the wire fence. 'Come on.'

'Where's your mate these days? He hasn't been in for ages?' Murphy says, dropping to the ground with a thump.

'Houston? Hibernating. He takes to the bed,' Mann says.

'Do you have fags?' he says to Corless.

'One. You a lighter? '

'I'll get a few drags off ya. Come on, I'm dying for one.' Mann says and they walk off down the winding track to the thicker clusters of trees near the old convent wall.

I do listen sometimes in classes. Mainly in English, but when Mrs Morahan starts on about predicate and stuff like that, I find myself drifting to the yard outside. One day, I see Marley come out a window high up on the pebble dashed wall of the main building. He climbs down the drainpipe. Miss Tuohy looks out, her face a deep red. She reaches out and tries to drag him back in, but he calmly descends the pipe. The rest of the class notice and Mrs Morahan goes to the window.

'He has a lot of problems, that lad,' she says.

Today we are doing *The Merchant of Venice*. I am interested in getting to the part where the guy's leg will be cut off. I'm not sure if that happens but I heard something about a pound of flesh being owed.

We each get to read parts. Melvin, much to his annoyance, must read for Gratiano. He speaks the lines with an inanimate tone, like a fridge humming. I enjoy reading in class. I am given Bassanio, a small part but better than Nerissa, who has hardly any lines it seems, or Servant.

'*I oft found both: I urge this childhood proof,*' I read, '*Because what follows is pure innocence...*' now a tooth

80

bugging me for a while falls out and my mouth fills with blood. My cheeks are puffed out.

'Mmm…mmm.' I say.

'Sorry, what was that?' Mrs Morahan is confused. I wave desperately and leave the classroom. I spit two cheekfuls of blood into a sink in the prefab jacks. The baby tooth floats around in the red sea before swirling down the plughole. The jacks look as though there was a violent reprisal for squealing when I am finished.

One day, I wake up with a rotten flu. My throat feels like there is wire wool tacked to the sides. It is insanely difficult to get out of my bed. Our house is central heated, there are no fires on in the morning and it is freezing. My socks are stuck together with frost, I guess. Conveniently, it is snowing outside. I have a particular nasty ten minutes waiting for the bus during which I think I will die. It occurs I could have taken the day off sick. I don't take days off sick, for some reason. Dad always says you should try and go in, if at all possible. The thought of returning to my warm bed is just becoming inviting, when Mad-dog swerves around the corner. I am freezing when I get to school and the ice box art room at the end of the prefabs is no addition. I rub my legs constantly to keep warm.

I have a booming headache and my nose is blocked. At lunchtime, I walk along the corridor by the senior classrooms. Martin Ainsworth pops out a doorway and swings his fist toward my balls.

'Stop that!' I growl, glaring at him. He stares at me, his eyes water. He turns away and goes back into room thirteen.

After Easter, the weather clears up. The end of the year is getting closer. I feel an excitement in the pit of my stomach. To be away from the First Year status, smallest of the small, there to be picked on, to be humiliated, often by your own peers.

One day, I say 'Hello' to Alannah as we wait for the German teacher. She says 'Hello,' back.

Perhaps someday we may even have a conversation. But I won't get carried away. I watch *Home and Away* every evening, marvelling at the ease the male characters speak to the females.

The weather gets very warm, girls take off their jumpers, the blue blouses show the track of the bra. Sometimes they don't wear tights. Keadin stands near me one day at the complex doors, looking across the yard at a line of girls sitting on the low wall at the end of the yard.

'What do you think, Brush?' he says.

'What's that?' I say. Keadin's face is now covered in peeling spots, along with his weight problems, I feel sorry for him. I assume he is not asking me about his largest zit. He nods over at the wall, I follow his gaze.

'See the gap?'

'What gap?' I say, puzzled.

I look over, Rebecca sits amongst them, a flash of flesh between skirt and blouse knotted at the end, her blonde hair down over her chest. She wears clear tights.

'In between the legs. The darkness.' Keadin smiles, then licks his lips.

Rebecca's skirt is flat across her thighs. I look between them as per Keadin, up to the black triangle.

82

I have not played much football during the year, but there are one or two injuries and Mr O' Leary, the manager, tells me I am in the squad for an away match. We take a minibus from the school at nine o'clock in the morning. Being on the squad has many advantages, not least the missing of a number of classes. There is the option of buying things in the shop and the craic on the bus. It is all First Years, so the hierarchal headaches are dispensed with. The only drawback is there are no girls anywhere to be seen. Mann is the goalkeeper. Quirke, Farrell and O'Brien are on the squad from my usual associates. Neither Carvey nor the captain Jimmy Moran have turned up today, much to our coach's fury. Conway was a good player, it is said, but is too weak. Melvin is strong in training and can kick the ball hard, but unfortunately not in any specific direction. Most of the team are flatheads from room eight and ten, they are so educationally attentive and uninteresting socially, I barely know their names. On the way, the lads are hyped up, released from the shackles of the classroom.

'I can hypnotise people,' Mann announces. I sit next to him, in front of the back row. 'Hey Brush, I'll hypnotise you.'

'It's alright,' I say.

'Ah come on, Brush, for the craic,' Farrell goads, in the Daddy seat for the day.

'Cone on Mann, let's see it,' Carvey adds.

'Do it!' Quirke concludes.

'Okay, look at me, Brush,' Mann says. I relent, the crowd of boys now around me.

'Look closely into my eyes,' Mann says. I look closer into his eyes.

'Closer,' Mann says, his face near mine. I smell toothpaste. I am impressed by this. Then I realise it is probably a smoking-related counter subterfuge.

His nose is now a few millimetres from mine. He stares at me. I do not feel in any way hypnotised. The lads are silent. Mr O'Leary will be wondering what is going on, the only sound the humming of the bus engine underneath us.

Crack! Mann rams his forehead against the top of my nose.

'Uhgh, ya cunt!' I say, leaning back. The lads erupt in laughter.

'That'll put you to sleep!' Mann says, guffawing like a jackass.

'Funny,' I say. I should give him a good fucking clout, but he's still a big bastard. I curse myself for letting it happen.

We tog out while Mr O'Leary gives us a pep talk. 'Don't be afraid to give them a few whips,' he says.

I am on the bench. Things do not go well. We are losing by eighteen points at half time.

'Lads, what did I say to ye?' Mr O'Leary marches around the dressing room.

'But they're all a foot taller than us,' one of the flat heads murmurs.

'Don't mind that. You're going on for the second half, corner forward,' Mr O'Leary turns to me. 'Take over from Philip. Remember – no fucking chances. Give it to them!' Mr O'Leary seems to have had a brain transplant, from a mild mannered maths teacher, to a blood thirsty commander.

The game is not a success for me. I do not touch the ball. I do get a slap across the head at one stage from my marker when the ball comes near me, before he takes it and kicks it up field.

'Get fucking stuck in,' Mr O'Leary howls from the line. We do reduce the deficit at full time, only losing by thirteen points.

'It's going to be a long five years for this team,' are Mr O'Leary's parting words in the dressing room. As we walk out of the clubhouse, the player I was marking jostles past me.

'Get off me,' I say, pushing him forward, sick of the whole lot of it. He swings around.

'You little cunt,' he says, even though he is the same size as me. We mutually conclude that a clash must happen. My eyes widen, everything through the year, Martin Ainsworth, Carvey, Mann's fucking hypnotism, the bastard pulling my ponytail seems to explode inside and I launch at the player, spraying belts at him. I can't see him, I just punch constantly, like Schwarzenegger in *Commando*, one blow after another, 'attack is the best form of defence' is the mantra in my mind. It seems to work, as the player, despite probably being fitter and more nimble than me, can't get his hands near my face, although, disappointingly after some minutes of this, there is not much of a mark on him either. The other team's coach comes out and the player runs off, giving me the finger.

'Fuck you,' I say, breathless. Coins have fell from my pocket out on the ground. I start picking them, my fingers shaking all over the place. Quirke picks up some and hands them to me.

'You had him, Brush. He's a dirty bastard anyway. He was going for your balls the whole time, there.'

'Good scrappin' though,' Brush,' Farrell says.

'Yeah, O'Leary would be proud of you' Mann says, bounding again to an imaginary beat.

85

Mr O'Leary arrives outside.

'What the hell is going on here? Get onto the bus!'

'Hey, hey,' Mac says, as the students dash up the corridor, the bell has rang at four o'clock on May 31st, the last day of the school year.

'Hello, Second Years,' a Second Year girl says, leaning over the stairs handrail at Peter F. Shylock's office.

'Hello Inter Cert-ulp!' I say, as The Principal emerges from his lair, carrying a bunch of keys. He does not look impressed with this unnecessary ribaldry.

We push and shove as we try to get out the entrance porch, it is like everyone wants to leave as quickly as possible, even the flat-heads. At the bus queue, Needham runs up with an open box of eggs and flings several at Conway. The eggs splatters squarely on Conway's jumper, Carvey follows with a bag and dusts the poor bastard in flour, to roars of approval. The pair run off to another bus before Conway can even think of retribution.

'Get onto the bus, for Christ's sake, ing,' Mad-dog growls.

Freddy Fanning and Quirke's brother are staging an arm-wrestling tournament near the back of the bus. The twins are a model of contrast, Jimmy chats with Rebecca laughing amongst the girls' seats, swigging a bottle of coke sloppily, a cigarette in his mouth as Mad-dog speeds down the avenue, Joseph, unmoving, sits beside Conway, staring blankly into the void between the two seats ahead. Quirke, Farrell and O'Brien discuss the summer's football with the parish.

'We play a few matches tonight, down at the school,' I say to Melvin.

'Yeah. But it's a bit risky now, evenings are very bright.'

'Oh yeah, we were bringing in bales until nine o'clock last night,' Conway chirps from behind.

'Did ye get them all in?' Melvin says, turning around. I lose interest and eavesdrop on the back row, soon to be released forever.

'We're nearly away from this old sardine can,' Sands announces.

'Are you forgetting that old exam next month?' Cigar puts in.

'I'm driving down for that, I've th' oul' lad's car,' Marcus says.

'Come on lads, a song,' Sands roars, belting Crazy in the ribs. The trainee human rights protester growls and wraps his arm around Sands' neck.

'Come on The Reds, come on The Reds!' The back row chant. The Daddy bangs the back window in warped tune with the singing. Mad dog looks in his large rear-view mirror with distaste.

'Come on The Reds, come on The Reds!'

'Tits, fanny, United, and The Reds go marching on, on, on!

The year is finally over. There is something of elation as I walk past the swinging door panels, taking a last look at Mad-dog as he scratches a boil on his neck, his face red, his shirt soaked in seat from the summer heat.

There is an ambulance at the front door. It starts up and drives out past me. Mam and dad are getting into the car. It's something to do with gran. There seems to be a hurry on them, so I don't bother going into the house. I squash my 'Jack's Army' schoolbag against the back window of the car as dad drives towards the county town.

II

The light fades. The bicycles pull up on the grassy drive. Doyle takes a folded piece of paper from his green coat.

'I made a floor plan. To see where the best place would be for access.'

The boy and Melvin nod. The three walk around the building to the back. There is a small yard with piles of rusting iron, rotten wooden pallets, a gate overgrown with nettles into the field beyond.

'This was the store room,' Doyle says, reading from the sheet. 'Let's tackle that big window there.'

Doyle pulls a long plank from the side of the yard and starts beating the glass.

'Tough as fuck,' he says after a number of blows.

The glass finally cracks. The boy takes up a rock and smashes the window to pieces.

'Good work,' Doyle says.

They climb in the window. For years the boy had watched Doyle and Melvin scale trees like monkeys, while he stood rooted to the ground, fearing a fall. Now he is growing, he is stronger, he can climb too, as well as them, perhaps soon better than them. There is a damp smell inside. Doyle waves his flash lamp.

'Careful,' Melvin says looking out at the road. 'I think the flash lamp is risky. If Agnes' mother looked across the fields, she'd see the lights.'

'Fuck it, if anyone comes, we'll run, sure they'll never catch us. Anyway, that oul' biddy is in bed since ten,' Doyle says.

'Why did you want to come in here again?' the boy says.

'Might be useful stuff.'

'Like what, though?' Melvin says, looking around, taking up a decapitated hammer handle.

The shop counter has cardboard boxes of obsolete engine parts. A cash register lies in the middle, old fashioned numbers on its display. The boy imagines ancient transactions taking place. He swipes the cash register to the ground.

'Hey! That might have been working,' Doyle says, rushing over.

The boy walks over to an aisle unit of shelves. Within damp cardboard boxes, he finds rusted nuts, bolts, iron hooks.

'Pure shit,' the boy says. He pushes over the unit. The items tumble out.

'What's wrong with ya? Someone will hear,' Doyle says.

'We better get the fuck out of here,' Melvin says.

'Look, a washing machine motor,' Doyle says, standing at a wall, looking through a large container. He takes up the motor and examines it. The boy is not interested in the motor. He enjoyed knocking the unit, invading the thoroughfare of the old shop.

A car pulls up outside, drives near the door. Doyle turns off his flash lamp.

'Fuck, get down on the floor,' Doyle whispers.

The boy lies down. The ground is moist, dust goes in his nose. He likes the smell.

'Don't move,' Doyle hisses. The car engine idles, the door opens.

There are footsteps on the gravel outside. The footsteps come nearer. A shape moves across the front windows. The footsteps move away. The car door closes. The car drives off.

'That was too fucking close,' Doyle says.

'Smoking is prohibited anywhere in or around the school and coming to and from the school in uniform. New pupils should familiarise themselves with the advice in the homework diary.' Peter F. Shylock announces to the lines of pupils in the assembly hall the following Monday. Tiny First Years with fresh new uniforms line the wall to the boy's left.

The advice in the homework diary now seems to him ambitious, if not in fact insane. Four hours a night was a good theory, but one he has never put into regular practice. He does not do homework. His summer report was marginally better than the Christmas one. Mr Kirk passed him this time but he slipped to a D in Maths and a C in English. He feels he is pushing against a powerful wave at the seaside, and it will be easier to wait for the waves to stop coming, than to halt their progress.

He sees Alannah in the line ahead. He observes her golden hair, tied differently this year. He notices her looking toward the large windows. Perhaps she is looking back to see if he is looking at her. At one stage she does look back, he thinks she caught his eyes, but she looks forward again. It warms him.

They are assigned Room Twenty-Two upstairs. Most of the same students from Room Ten are still in the class. Corless has been transferred from the room nine group. He tells them that he, Mann and Houston's habit of throwing spare chairs at each other during Mr Fogarty's class had possibly led to Peter F. Shylock deciding they should be separated. But Corless does not seem to the boy to be too much of a trouble-maker.

He says little after the initial explanation of his arrival at first break, leaning quietly against the radiator at the blackboard behind the teacher's table. The classroom has a line of windows over the top of the inside wall along the corridor, possibly to accommodate Peter F. Shylock observing any antics easily. In the corner are shelves for the schoolbags. The external windows look out across the yard and the tennis courts. The boy can see the First Years in the prefabs below, finding their seats, their friends, their way. He feels superior.

The teachers are mostly the same. Mrs Morahan takes Second Year English. The boy grimly reflects he will miss out again on the newspaper-making exercises of the other English teacher, but he doesn't really care anymore. He continues to make newspapers and magazines at home, no one reads them, but he likes to make them anyway.

Rebecca Joyce sits at the other end of the classroom, the boy is no longer behind her. But some other girls sit near him. He imagines shifting some of them. It is easier to talk to the less attractive girls, there is less fear of humiliation. Aine says 'Hello' to him, another says 'Welcome back Brush.'

In the morning on the yellow bus, there had been some confusion with the seating arrangements. Some of the First Years didn't seem to understand the hierarchy that was in place and the boy sat quite far up.

He will not let that happen this evening. Mad-dog scowls as the boy gets on early. The Weasel is already on his throne, there was never any doubt he would rule, at least on the yellow bus, whatever about the school, and the rumoured reservations of some other Leaving Certs, such as Martin Ainsworth.

The boy sits beside Melvin who has taken the fourth seat back across from Quirke and Farrell.

'What did you make of Corless?' the boy says to Melvin.

'Sound enough,' Melvin says.

'This year will be a bit easier, I'd say. Timetable is not too bad, apart from double French on Monday morning – hey!' A small piece of paper hits the boy on the head. It has come from up the bus, one of the First Year seats of all places. One of them laughs, a small spotty boy.

'Did you throw that?' the boy shouts up. 'Fucking First Years, throwing shit down here, ya little prick, if I get ya doin' that again, you're dead!' the First Year looks down at the boy, his face blank.

'Sit down,' Freddy Fanning says to the First Year, as he comes down the aisle.

He stops at the boy's seat. 'What the fuck are you doing, Brush?'

'Uh?' the boy says.

'I said, what the fuck are you doing?'

'What?'

'You're in my bag's seat.'

'What?'

'I said...' Freddy Fanning looks at the boy coldly. 'You're in my bag's seat.'

The boy looks around. Freddy Fanning's seat is the second row from the back, he sat there in the morning and shared cigarettes with the new Daddy.

'Ha-ha…yeah right,' the boy says, looking ahead. Freddy Fanning puts his index finger and his thumb on the boy's neck and pushes the boy's head toward his knees.

'I said…' the boy smells cowshit on Freddy Fanning's fingers, 'That's my fucking bag's seat.'

'Uh…Okay…,' the boy says, his lips brushing against his teeth.

The boy's eyes water as Freddy Fanning squeezes tighter. A lot of the bus students are watching, the boy can hear intermittent murmurs replacing chatter.

'Get the fuck up there on Melvin's knees.'

Then the grip is released. The boy slowly clambers up onto Melvin's wide thighs. He pushes his back against the window. Only the girls ever sit on each other's knees. He glances slowly up the bus. Rebecca is looking back at him sitting on Melvin's lap. Another girl whispers something, giggles, they both laugh. The boy stares at Frederick Fanning's small orange bag on the seat outside, just one exercise book and a lunchbox behind the loose straps.

'You didn't know that was Freddy's brother?' Melvin says as the boy nears home, after most of the back row have gotten off.

'No. Jesus, what a prick, that Fanning is,' the boy says.

'Don't mind him. He's sound enough most of the time.'

'Yeah, we had him doing silage, drawing for us, and he was sound as a bell,' Conway says from across the aisle.

94

The first couple of days he stands in the yard with Quirke, Farrell and O'Brien but their conversations bores him, they centre on homework, parish matches, football in England. Liverpool F.C. are in decline and he has no wish to talk soccer with Farrell and Quirke about the rise of their Manchester United. He now chooses to spend the breaks in Room Twenty-Two, leaning against the radiator at the teacher's table with Melvin, Conway and Corless.

Corless loves Mr Bean on television. The boy has not seen it yet. Corless describes the things Mr Bean does with credit cards and hot water bottles. Corless looks like he will explode with laughter. The boy thinks it is funny but it would be funnier if he had seen it, yet he laughs, he laughs intensely.

Needham, Carvey, Mann and Houston, often visit from room eighteen, where the old room nine class has moved to, next door to Peter F. Shylock's office.

'Howye girls,' Needham says. The smell of tobacco is strong.

'Move over there,' Carvey says at the radiator, pushing the boy over. The boy should push back he knows, but he is still smaller than Carvey, who seems to have grown even more.

The boy sees Doyle walking around the school during the first weeks. He looks hilariously small in the corridors, the boy thinks, without his green woollen cap, his BMX bike, his flash lamp. Stripped of his accessories, he looks like a child. The boy barely recognises him.

First and Second Years do not fraternise generally. Doyle sits on the bus with two First Years from the village, McNulty and Ford. Conversations with the boy are usually

95

held outside of school on Friday night at the village school yard, or at the boy's house, in the new TV room. The room was converted after his grandmother died in June, a shelf put in the corner, the bed she slept in taken away, the couch from the living room positioned in its place. Doyle comes in the window in the evenings and they watch *Minder* and play *Sonic the Hedgehog*. Doyle finally gets through to the uncharted territory of the second level, Bridge Zone. He is so excited, he spends hours trying to negotiate its hidden traps. Doyle does not seem to care the boy wants to go to bed at half eleven. In the morning the boy is cranky, the sky is dark, the school day is a tortuous process to be gotten through.

After Hallowe'en the classes are split into Honours and Pass in some subjects. For maths, the boy joins Quirke, Farrell and O'Brien to go downstairs to room eleven. Carvey, Needham, Mann and Houston arrive upstairs, joining Melvin, Conway and Corless. The boy finds honours maths very tedious even though Rebecca and Alannah are there. He does not know why he is doing honours maths when he got a D in his report. Mr O'Leary said he should do honours, if he could at all. But the class bores him. He is walking down the stairs to it one day when he meets Carvey.

'Where are you going, Brush? Not doing maths?'

'I'm in honours,' the boy says.

'Oh, "I'm in honours,"' Carvey mimics. 'Well, I don't like people in honours. Fucking swots,' Carvey says. 'And I don't like that haircut, I'm going to cut off that girl's tail one of these days.' He smacks the boy on the back of the head and walks off. The honours class gets more difficult. The boy looks out the window, across the yard, beyond the tennis courts, to the trees, to the clouds beyond.

One day when Quirke, Farrell and O'Brien get up to go to room eleven for honours maths, the boy stays in his seat. After a few minutes, Needham and company arrive. Needham fits a tennis racket cover on his head and dances on top of one of the desks in front. Mann and Carvey start a light-hearted wrestling match. Houston and Corless count cigarettes.

'Are you not going down to maths?' Melvin says to the boy.

'Nah, I'll sit here and enjoy the show,' the boy says and laughs.

The pass class moves at a much more leisurely pace. He does not tell his parents about the change. He also decides to move to pass commerce, and Irish has been given up on. He still attends the foundation class, taught by Mr Fogarty and works on drawing the new Liverpool FC crest.

He decides to further develop the antics of the pass class, their tennis racket cover wearing, their banging of desk covers, their throwing around of chairs. He discovers that the desk lids will come off if pushed hard enough. It is not enough to loosen them, now he wants to break them, he finds. He initiates a game of cricket with Mann during Miss Tuohy's French class. Mann tosses a piece of paper toward him while Miss Tuohy writes on the board and he tries to bat it with his pencil case at her. It misses, bouncing against the board. Miss Tuohy swings around to an expressionless class. The boy enjoys the irritation on her face.

In wet November mornings, he clambers out to his parents' bedroom at seven. He tells his mother he has pains in his stomach, or a headache, or a sore throat, she nods in agreement. He returns to the warmth of the bed, covering himself over, dreaming of another place, with Alannah or Rebecca, away from the cold torment of the yellow bus, enjoying its engine snorting past outside, away from the pressure of the groups in the school, the pressure of everything.

Some cliques have merged together in the Second Year. Mann has joined with Needham and Carvey. Houston is rarely at school now, and Corless spends most of his time in Room Twenty-Two, standing at the radiator with Melvin and Conway, laughing until he cries about the antics of Mr Bean. Needham leads Carvey and Mann in various zany actions, trying to run up walls, hanging from the underside of stair threads. Sometimes the boy joins them, sometimes he stays with the others at the radiator, trying to pull it off its brackets.

There is a silence between Farrell and the boy now, they do not talk in good humoured rivalry about Liverpool and Manchester United anymore, the boy does not know why. Farrell sometimes elbows him at the bag shelves at four o'clock. The boy elbows him back.

Only the old room eight crew of Ryan, Keadin, Keegan and Murphy seems to have survived, they lounge around in Room Eleven, home of the saints, the boy thinks of it, where honours classes are held. This group seem more mature, Ryan has a girlfriend much older, she is in Fourth Year, he plays music in a pub band, his father lets him drive to school. Murphy is not to be found at the trees anymore, now when the boy passes room eleven at breaks, he sees him reading a book. Keadin and Keegan stand soberly at the windows, hands in pockets, one leg bent, the other flat. The posture of an adult. The boy is irritated.

The boy's 'Jack's Army' schoolbag goes missing on the bus. He left it as usual at his feet when he sat down and while talking to Farrell about something it had disappeared. He walks up and down the aisle.

Eventually he risks checking the back row. He casually stops in front of The Weasel, carefully leaning forward, looking along each side. Smoke from The Weasel's cigarette stings his eye. The yellow and green bag is under the seat in front of another leaving cert.

'Oh, there it is,' the boy says.

'It's alright there,' The Weasel says, warmly. 'I'll look after it.'

It is clear the schoolbag cannot be retrieved. The boy walks back to his seat, hoping the damage will be minimal. Later in the journey, there is a bang on the roof. He looks back. Freddy Fanning is throwing the boy's football boots repeatedly against the thin steel shell.

'Who-hoy!' The back row chorus each impact.

Bang! 'Who-hoy!'

Bang! 'Who-hoy!

The boy looks up the aisle, seeing Rebecca looking back, he wonders if she knows the items are his.

Mad-Dog pulls up the bus. He gets out of his seat. This has happened less this term. There were many instances the previous year when Mad-dog came down, threatening Marcus with expulsion from Bus Eireann services, searching the seats for cigarettes, to jeers.

This year he seems less bothered, even with the strong smell of cigarette smoke, Mad-dog usually focusses on the fields zipping past, the peaceful sheep dotted in the landscape.

Today, he comes to the gathering of Freddy Fanning, The Weasel and Quirke's brother, who has joined in the fun.

'What's going on here, ing?' What are ye doing with them boots, ing?' Mad-dog says to Freddy Fanning.

'What boots?' Freddy Fanning says. The boots lie in front of him. 'I don't know about any boots, Jack,' Freddy Fanning says.

The boy hurries down to the aisle. 'They're mine, Jack,' the boy says. The 'Jack's Army' schoolbag is tied in hundreds of little knots around the back of a seat. He tries to untangle them.

'I told you I'd look after it,' The Weasel says, his high-pitched voice stinging.

'Get off my bus,' Mad-dog says to The Weasel. 'You as well,' he says to Freddy Fanning.

'What? We didn't do anything?' Freddy Fanning says.

'Ye took his fucking bag and threw the stuff all over the place. Now that's improper conduct, ing? I might ban ye altogether yet, if ye don't get the fuck off, now!' Mad-dog roars, his face turning purple. The boy progresses slowly through the intricate design of restraint The Weasel had engineered.

'I done nothing,' The Weasel says.

'You just said you did to him, now git the fuck off!'

The Weasel and Freddy Fanning slowly get up and walk past Mad-Dog. 'We're five miles from home,' Freddy Fanning says, swinging his school bag around his shoulder.

'Ye should have thought of that before ye started acting the bollocks!' Mad-dog says as the boy finally untangles the last knot, pulls the school bag up and walks back up the aisle.

As Mad-Dog drives off, the boy watches Freddy Fanning and The Weasel walking along the road, their faces grim and grey.

Conway is not at school the next day. Melvin talks to the boy on the bus home.

'There was a fella near Conway wrapping round bales until eleven last night,' Melvin says. 'They came over and asked me to draw in for them. I was driving their Super Ford. It's a great yoke.'

'Pity you couldn't drive them on the road,' the boy says.

'You can if you're sixteen and have the licence,' Melvin says.

'That'd be great,' the boy says. He visualises the four wheels, the accelerator lever pulled back, the rev of the engine loud in front of him, twisting the steering wheel around bends. The ability to go wherever he might choose. 'I'd love to get–,' the boy stops as sharp wood sinks at pace into his shoulder.

'Thanks, Jimmy,' Freddy Fanning says, handing a T-square to Jimmy Moran. The pain travels along the boy's shoulder to his neck and down his arm. He realises then it was Freddy Fanning, sitting at an angle beside O'Brien, who pulled his ponytail all the previous year, who smacked him on the skull when the long hair was out of reach.

'Ouch!' Melvin says, smiling. 'But they all go without any paperwork,' Melvin continues the conversation, as if nothing had happened, as if no boundary had been breached.

The German teacher is late. The boy is sitting next to Alannah. He likes sitting next to her. She writes her name with a large A. He calculates how many letters of her name are in his. He is watching her write, when someone laughs behind him, He looks around. A few of the girls are giggling. Someone mutters 'Alannah is going with The Brush.'

'Are you, Alannah?' one of the girls says.

'I don't know,' Alannah says, not looking up from her book. He imagines her now, the one day she looked straight at him in the class. It was like a form of hypnotism. The contrast between her soft brown eyes and Mann's hard green dots on the minibus is sickening to him. Sickening that he cannot say anything to Alannah, just persist in trying to touch her elbow with his, again and again, he tries it.

P.E. class follows German and the boy runs into the complex, where Miss Tuohy drags a large plastic bag of balls. For some reason, he grabs the bag off her. He ignores her high-pitched cries of complaint, he opens the bag, the balls fall out, there are all types: volleyballs, tennis balls, footballs, basketballs, a rugby ball. He kicks the balls all over the complex, out the fire exit, at the roof as hard as he can, one gets satisfactorily jammed between a Perspex sheet and a roof girder.

It is the type of thing Needham was said to do last year, it is the type of thing he wants to do now, he laughs, he loves the madness of it, the badness of it. The balls roll in all directions, Miss Tuohy screams and chases him around the complex as he carries the half-empty bag of balls, the class laughs, Rebecca is laughing too, he guesses. Miss Tuohy catches his jumper, they twirl around like haphazard dancers, he pulls off the jumper, Miss Tuohy is chasing the empty jumper now, he runs off, it's hilarious for everyone except the teacher, the class is a great success, one that will live long in the memory.

There is a heavy fall of snow. Mad-dog growls at the wipers as the boy gets on the bus. The tree branches which scrape the roof every morning leave fine white dust on the road in the bus' wake. The boy rubs his hands to warm them. His mother had given him purple woollen gloves but he places them in his schoolbag.

At the school, everything is coated in a thin white blanket. When the boy steps out, Farrell tosses a snowball at him, it breaks gently against his jacket. He fires one back, his aim is not good. He does not aim in fact, he finds himself closing his eyes, not even looking where he throws, just putting the energy into throwing it. It falls harmlessly on the ground, a good distance from Farrell. He feels fear as he walks to the entrance porch, as though on a battlefield. There is a snap as something hits Conway on the back of the head. A stone rolls on the ground, still half within its snow shell. Conway staggers and sits against the low windowsill.

'Jesus, he's fucking concussed,' Farrell says.

'Better tell Mac,' O'Brien says, arriving.

'Dirty cunts,' Farrell says, looking down the avenue. Marley and O'Toole walk in a side door.

In January, the boy notices he has gotten taller. He can see the mirror in the bathroom. For years, he had looked up to this mirror, he could see his reflection. He does not remember his whole face becoming visible bit by bit in the glass. It is like just now he can see himself, now he can see all his face. There is no hair around his jaw yet. He has decided to stop wearing the ponytail. He will wear his hair loose around his shoulders from now on. He notices it move in the shadows around his silhouette in the sunlight evenings, as he walks to the bus. It covers his skull, it imprints something else on the ground, something different to him. He likes to do this. He wants to do it more.

Quirke, Farrell and O'Brien stand below at the complex, talking, he guesses about the weekend sport. The parish team are in the county semi-final. In England, Manchester United are top of the league, Liverpool are having a disappointing season. The boy waits with Melvin and Conway. Corless is absent much of the time. Sometimes Mann and Houston, who has made a reappearance in the new term, arrive. Despite his lengthy sabbatical, Houston remains sleepy-eyed, low-toned, sluggish in his movements.

'Got a fag, Mann?' he whispers often. They talk about lifting heavy weights. Mann says that his cousin could lift a cement bag over his head when he was four years old. They discuss the viability of such a claim for some time.

The boy gets bored and looks out a window. Near the wire fence, Alannah and two friends walk along. She slows in the midst of them, spreading her hands by her sides, out from her hips slightly, her head down. She is telling them something, he guesses. Then they walk on again.

'It couldn't pull the Zetor,' Conway is saying, there is a funny comment, everyone is laughing, he laughs too.

'Hey Brush, do you want a sweet?' Mann says.

The boy takes a soft jelly. He looks around, no one else is taking one.

'I don't know should you have done that,' Conway says, with a wise expression.

'Feeling funny?' Mann says, a smirk on his face, similar to the way he smiled before he head-butted the boy on the minibus. Mann has not got any taller, the boy is nearly his height now, but Mann seems to have grown out more, he is heavier. The boy is closer now to Carvey's height too, but Needham has grown further, his thin frame lanks over the others.

A tingling sensation comes over the boy. The others stand around him in a circle, observing him like a he is a strange animal.

'Feel like a bit of ass, Brush?' Mann says and guffaws, the others laugh too.

Later, Quirke tells him it was a mail order sweet, claiming to make people amorous. It did not work. The boy thinks he has no need of potions to feel that way. What annoys him is why he was chosen to be the sampler, why he would be the one they would laugh at, they would humiliate.

Mac calls him over in the corridor one day. 'Hey, hey, you have been missing a lot of days,' The Vice Principal looks in his blue folder. 'Twenty-three so far this year. Is there something wrong at home?'

'No sir,' the boy says.

'You don't have any serious illness?'

'No, sir.'

'Right. We'll bring it up at the parent-teacher meeting, okay.' Mac writes in his blue folder, the conversation is over.

The parent-teacher meeting is held midway through the spring term. The news is not good, the boy is not performing in any class, even English. At this rate he will fail all his subjects. As usual, it is said he has tons of ability but appears to have no interest in using it. The boy says nothing as the outcome is relayed to him at the door of the TV room. He changes channels as though he is not there, not listening. He is somewhere else, somewhere far away.

On his days off, when he is sick, there is a great freedom. He eat coco-pops at ten o'clock and listens to *The Gay Byrne Show*. He loves the jingle that pre-empts the advertisements.

He creates newspapers at the kitchen table, recording news on the radio bulletin and forming them into reports.

This is what he should be doing at school he thinks. The nucleus of room eight, now in room eleven, are still getting to make weekly newspapers. His class continue to do the accursed verb word search, study passages from *Tom Brown's Schooldays*.

The boy decides to create a competition for the rest of the class to guess how many days he has missed. Everyone must pay a pound and the correct answer, if there is one, will receive twenty pounds. If everyone participates, it will mean a profit of ten pounds if someone guesses or thirty pounds if no one guesses right. The answer is actually thirty-one but the boy decides to claims it is sixty-three. The boy circulates the entry form. Someone guesses sixty-three.

In the middle of Mrs Sharpe's class, she notices the boy handing the sheet to Orla. Mrs Sharpe takes it up and reads it quickly. She tears it into small pieces. The boy is sickened, the monies are returned, the competition abandoned.

Mrs Sharpe also teaches them guidance, skipping over the chapter on sex. She ignores the boy for the most part, turns her attention to the girls in the class. One day, she sees Orla talking to Rebecca, whispering.

'You girl, stand,' Mrs Sharpe says.

Orla stands slowly. 'What was the conversation you were having there?'

'Nothing, miss. '

'I said, what was the conversation you were having there?'

'Nothing, miss.' Oral stands awkwardly, at a slant. She is still small relative to the class. Everyone looks at her. Mrs Sharpe turns her lips sourly and prods the table with a clipped fingernail. Orla is red in the face. Her glassed protect her eyes, but the boy senses there are tears welling.

Mrs Sharpe leaves Orla standing for the rest of the class. Mrs Sharpe is evil, the boy decides. But even he would not disrupt her class.

Mr Fogarty follows. He does not speak much with the class anymore about going shopping or the price of electricity. He seems tired. He reads from the text books at the teacher's table. The class breathe, shouting, jumping, using up the energy distilled during Mrs Sharpe's class.

Later, a rumour goes around about Orla that she is dripping blood. Everywhere the boy sees her, she is blushing. He looks at her skirt, there is no blood. But he hears she is leaking it.

'Had the period in home economics,' Ryan announces at the complex doors. 'Spat it all over the place. Nearly poisoned the fucking teacher's buns.'

'There'll be extra strawberry sauce on Pete's dessert today,' Needham adds metallically.

Orla comes out through the prefab doors.

'Bloody, bloody, bloody!' The chant rises, gaining power.

The boy roars the word with the others, feeling the syllables; 'Bl-oo-dy,' enjoying the power of it, the colour of it, the searching redness.

The German class is becoming miserable for him. He has made no more progress with Alannah. He enjoyed the thought that she had encouraged him the day she said 'she didn't know' if she was going out with him, but fantasising with a sock on Saturday mornings is as far as he has been able to bring this to his advantage. She actually moves her desk away from him, toward the window.

The class itself is a bore. He dreams now of driving a big tractor around the fields. He has driven his father's Massey Ferguson 35 a few times. It is a small tractor, as small as they come. It does not have lights, or much of a cab. His hands are still cold when he drives it, as they are on the bicycle. When he cycles to Melvin's in the evenings, he wonders what it would be like to drive the tractor there.

The boy talks to Melvin as he milks cows. At nine they go into Melvin's house. Mrs Melvin gives the boy ham sandwiches and treacle bread. Melvin's father is old, more than sixty. He sits at the kitchen table and always asks the boy one or two questions. What was he doing at the weekend? Does he help his father out? The boy says he cleans the cattle shed, clearing away dung with a scraper, or doses sheep or cattle. Sometimes these reports are true, but the boy finds himself exaggerating, embellishing his efforts to smoothen the conversation. Melvin's father nods and says 'Good man.'

Doyle's father is also old, and sometimes allows Doyle to drive his car. Doyle taps on the boy's bedroom window one night, as usual wearing his green woollen cap. To the boy, the green cap brings excitement, warmth, he is always happy to see Doyle, to enter into unpredictable territory.

'See what I have,' Doyle says. Doyle has parked at the edge of the shop forecourt.

'Don't want them asking questions,' Doyle says.

The car is a Ford Sierra. Doyle pronounces 'Sierra' 'Sigh-era', which the boy feels is wrong but he does not say anything. Doyle wants to demonstrate all of the car's features.

'It has speakers in every door,' Doyle says. 'I can adjust them from the steering wheel. Notice.' Doyle turns on and off the speakers. It does not matter to the boy about the positioning of the speakers. He hears the engine throbbing, sees the bonnet trembling, smells the oil.

'It has power steering,' Doyle says. The boy wants to move the wheel to see how it is with the power steering but Doyle prefers to keep turning the wheel around.

'Wait, I'll demonstrate,' Doyle says, blocking the boy's hand. The boy does not get the chance to feel the turn of the wheel.

'Central locking too. Automatic.' Doyle says, locking the car, clicking the keys smoothly. The indicator lights flash and the car is silent. The boy looks at the dark shape, breathless.

Most Friday nights now they spend at the boy's house. Melvin and Conway occasionally come on bicycles. Doyle usually uses his BMX, although his father sometimes allows him to drive up the car. They play football in the front garden by the outside light. The game is easy, the boy uses his siblings as goalkeepers. There is no pressure to play well, it is not taken seriously.

When he plays with the village team there is pressure to get on the team, to play well, to keep his place. He does keep his place but the village soccer team is very bad. They lose every match by an average of ten goals. The boy plays up front and usually scores the consolation.

Melvin and Doyle play sometimes for the soccer team. Quirke, Farrell and O'Brien play gaelic football for the parish. The boy is better at soccer than gaelic. You can punch people in the face in gaelic, as he has found out. He is not accurate with punches and usually gets punched first. This is not allowed in soccer. But there is no 'mass' on soccer, he has heard. All of the good players play for the parish. All of the players who can't get on the parish team play soccer. He is on the soccer team.

Playing soccer is no good at all, he knows. Being good at gaelic can get you a job working for the ESB or to get a permanent job as a teacher. The eldest of the Fannings, James, works for the ESB. Melvin says he got 'in' because he was good at playing Gaelic. Playing soccer will not get you a job for the ESB or Telecom Eireann or a permanent position as a teacher in a local school.

The boy tries out for the parish team. Quirke, Farrell and O'Brien are surprised to see him at the clubhouse.

'Givin' the Gah a go, Brush?' Quirke says.

They show him where to change, introduce him to the Under-16s coach, James Fanning. He smokes a Major as he tells the squad to run around the pitch twenty times. He sounds like Marcus, The Weasel and Freddy, he has the same strange high-pitched accent, a specific smooth tone. But this particular Fanning does not have the same method of inflicting pain. He prefers to demand press-ups, sprints, stretches, laps, through hailstones, howling icy wind, relentlessly.

During the practice sessions, the boy does not receive much of the ball. He has not played gaelic much in his childhood, they always played soccer in the village school even though this did not please the teachers. In the village school Quirke, Farrell, and O'Brien loved soccer. Now they will hardly discuss the sport, except when Manchester United have won.

At the first parish match, the boy is selected to play full forward. He does not touch the ball during the first half and is substituted. He scores a goal in training the following week. Farrell passes to him, he turns and hits the roof of the net. He relives this triumph for a number of nights. He feels perhaps he is good at gaelic.

Perhaps he could get to be a regular fixture on the parish team, like Quirke, Farrell and O'Brien and perhaps he could get a job with the ESB and drive a large truck to work every day like James Fanning. But when he is selected for the parish team the following Sunday, again he does not touch the ball. During one play, Jimmy Moran, one of the star players on the team runs with the ball. An opposing player tackles Jimmy. The boy backs away, free for the pass. But Jimmy gets caught in the opposing player and loses the ball.

'What the fuck are y'at, Brush, why didn't ya come up and give me a hand?'

'I was making room for the pass,' the boy says, but Jimmy is gone, tackling someone for the ball. He will never pass to him now, the boy thinks.

The games in the garden under streetlight are much more relaxed. The boy can organise the teams. Sometimes Doyle's older sister, Enid, comes and makes up the numbers. Doyle's sister is not really pretty, but the boy does not ever look at her like that, she is more like another sister. She looks too much like Doyle to be attractive. None of Doyle's sisters are attractive, they are masculine, muscular, with deep voices, while Doyle himself is fragile, weak, thin and speaks with a light voice.

Some nights the boy's parents go to the pub, or to meetings, or to courses, and the visitors can come in after the game for tea, biscuits and lemonade.

'Come on,' Doyle says urgently at the window, the woollen cap sliding down over his eyes.

'What are you on about, *Minder* is just starting?' the boy says.

'Come outside. You'll see,' Doyle says.

The boy climbs out the window. The night is silent, cool, dark. The Sierra ticks over on the side of the road.

'We call over to Melvin,' Doyle says. 'Th' oul' lad is in bed sick, he won't take any notice how long I'm gone.'

Doyle drives well. The car is comfortable. Doyle has music on too loud, the boy thinks. Doyle won't drive up to Melvin's house. He parks on the other side of the road, at a gate to a field. They walk into Melvin's yard. The boy enjoys the fact of not having cycled, not having got his hands cold,

112

his legs spattered from the puddles. The only thing missing is the pleasure of having drove.

Melvin is within the cow shed, milking as usual.

'How are ye lads?' Melvin says. 'How did ye come?' his usual question, as he sweeps the yard.

'By special transport, tonight,' the boy says. Wanting to show as much as Doyle, more than Doyle.

Doyle will not permit anyone else to drive the Sierra. He prefers to demonstrate his own driving.

Doyle drops the boy off at the house an hour later, in a hurry, suddenly nervous his father will notice how long it has taken to get milk at the shop.

Melvin does not visit very often now. The boy calls to him most evenings, talking to him in the milking parlour, watching Melvin attach the silver suction pumps to the cows' teats, sweeping channels clear of faeces and urine, hosing them with a pipe.

They talk about tractors and cars. Melvin's older brother, Dominic, has come home from England driving a Peugeot 505 with yellow number plates.

Melvin gets the keys one evening and they drive down the boreen at the side of Melvin's house. The boy cannot drive a car, has not really tried much, apart from one day, his father let him attempt to drive in the boreen to his grandmother's house. But he could not get the car to take off without letting the clutch up too fast and conking the engine.

'You failed,' his father said, as he grimly retook the driver's seat.

Melvin coaches the boy in driving. He must gently let the clutch out. He sees the keys of his mother's car one night, when they are gone to the pub. He goes out and sits in the driver's seat. He smells the plastic of the dash. It is a Toyota Corolla. He turns the key, red lights come on. He starts the engine. The body throbs under him. He drives it forward a couple of yards. He reverses it. He wonders if it is in the same place. He gets out. He will mark the spot the next time, if there is a next time. He tells his siblings he will beat them if they say anything. He adds he will bring them for a spin some night, too.

Other nights, Doyle comes on his bike and they play *Sonic the Hedgehog* or watch *Minder*. The boy loves watching Arthur Daley. He enjoys seeing Arthur get involved in various schemes. He would like a job like Arthur. He likes the idea of setting up a buy-and-sell business. He likes the hat Arthur wears. He finds a peaked farmer's cap his grandfather used to wear. He wears it when he cycles over to Melvin's. Always he wears this hat now, when not at school, it gives him something, he is not sure what.

The boy thinks about Arthur Daly a lot after the programme. Arthur goes to a pub where there is a stripper at lunchtime. The boy enjoys watching the scene of the stripper, even though nothing is shown apart from her shoulders and legs. There are no pubs with strippers where he lives. He wants to be Arthur Daley. A similar thing happened, he remembers, when he read the *Just William* books. He wanted to be William Brown. He remembers his mother saying, 'that was silly,' that William Brown was not real, he was 'plastic'. He remembers it clearly. Plastic.

'Come here,' Peter F. Shylock says to the boy, as he meekly files out after the new Summer term assembly.

'What is going on with you, hmm?' Peter F. Shylock says, looking closely at the boy. His face is nearly as close as Mann's was on the minibus, almost a year before. But The Principal's eyes are larger and darker than Mann's. 'Your report was poor again at Easter. The teachers tell me you are not participating in class. You seem to be in a world of your own. Yet they say you have ability. What is the problem here?'

'I don't know, sir.'

'You failed a number of subjects and you are doing pass now in nearly everything. Why don't you apply yourself a bit better, huh? Other fellas would be making a lot more of your ability, I can tell you.'

'I don't know sir.'

'You need to think about who you are hanging around with, huh?'

'Yes sir.'

'Get to class.'

The boy thinks about Peter F. Shylock. His breath was terrible. He stands very close to the person he speaks to, allowing hardly any personal space. The boy wonders why the teachers say he has ability. They seem exasperated with him most of the time.

Mrs Morahan was not pleased with his recent composition on Huckleberry Finn. He had not read the book since he was ten and summarised the blurb on the back cover.

'While well-written, there is no original work here. You can do better. D,' was the outcome. But this is more than the other subjects. Irish, he ignores completely. Mr Fogarty

115

has bought a new car, it reminds him of Kit in *Knight Rider*. A Mazda 323, a black with lift-up lights. Quirke says his brother heard Mr Fogarty is a 'lunatic' behind the wheel and has incurred numerous speeding tickets. The class still mostly ignore him, except when they want to know something about his vehicle. Rebecca Joyce is particularly interested.

'Does the roof come off, sir?' she says, tossing her blonde hair over the chair backrest. The boy imagines driving somewhere in Mr Fogarty's Mazda 323, Rebecca beside him, leaning into his chest, holding his hand.

Mr O'Leary struggles to explain theorems to the pass students; Carvey asleep, Corless picking his nose, Mann fondling his testicles. The boy is fascinated with the contrast in his humour on the football field from the classroom. He patiently dictates the ratio of pi at the blackboard while the boy pictures him launching a water bottle at one of the substituted players in the dug-out for missing an open goal.

'Fucking eejit,' Mr O'Leary growled then.

The French class is no better. Miss Tuohy still scowls at him. He relives the bag of balls incident with different groups of students, to hilarious guffaws and phrases of congratulations of a successfully disrupted class.

Some of the other girls in his class salute him often now in the corridor.

'Hi, Brush,' they say.

'Hello Karen,' he answers. 'Hello Joanne, Hello Eileen, Hello Mary.'

'How are you, Brush?'

He does not find any of these girls good looking. The lads call them dogs.

'She's an awful dog,' is the phrase most used.

There are a few couples in Second Year. One girl is said to be 'going out' with a tall freckled boy from inter cert. The boy sees them, walking, while holding hands discreetly in the assembly hall, talking at the far corner, watching the door for Peter F. Shylock, who does not approve of 'juvenile liaisons'.

Games tables have been introduced, the boy usually plays cards now with Melvin and Conway. He watches the couple chat from the card table. She leans her head on her boyfriend's chest. She rubs his arm. It does not look remotely sexual, the boy thinks. He wonders what they talk about. He wonders what they would do if it were to look remotely sexual.

Mann, Carvey and Needham are usually down in the trees smoking. Corless has not been in for weeks. 'James Corless,' is the automatic name volunteered when Mac calls to take the register. Officially, Corless is off sick. Mann says he is working in a garage. Houston is only in occasionally. The boy enjoys meeting Houston down at the assembly hall cloakroom, always the conversation is light, easy, unaffecting.

'Could have done with more of the bed today,' Houston mutters at the morning break, standing at the radiator in the darkness, amongst the coats, a sleepy tinge around his eyes.

'You spend your whole life in bed,' Mann snarls, trying to pull some hooks off the wall.

Mann says a lot of cutting things to Houston, but Houston never seems annoyed. The boy is puzzled, he thinks

Houston should respond, with something equally insulting, but he just laughs as well, laughing carelessly with Mann, who is laughing at Houston. The boy sometimes prefers to join these, declining the card game, the concentration required, the ignominy of losing, choosing the offbeat banter of the assembly hall cloakroom. Lots of students pass through. The Weasel arrives one day with another Leaving Cert, the boy worries he will get a slap, but The Weasel ignores him. A group of First Years wander in, their jumpers are still new looking, shirt collars drift over their jumpers, in the juvenile way. The boy's uniform seems smaller, he stretches his sleeves to his wrists.

Mann slaps some of the First Years across the head as they pass. 'Out of bounds, tits,' he shouts, toeing one of them in the rear as they leave.

An enterprise comes to the boy one day, while dreaming in the art room. He gathers up twenty large sheets, brings them to the assembly hall cloakroom, where the mechanical drawing class, who must order their sheets for ten pence in the drawing room, buy them off him for five pence. It is all profit. The boy's pockets jangle with change. Jimmy Moran gives him a pound coin for one sheet, it is twenty times the price, Jimmy does not seem to care. Jimmy always brings things from his father's shop to school, drumsticks, jelly tots, little bottles of Coca-Cola. His brother Joseph, who has grown much taller now than Jimmy, brings only water, ham sandwiches and water.

The new business runs well for two weeks. The boy has collected six pounds in change. Then it stops because of Marley and O'Toole.

'Ho Brush,' Marley says at the doorway. 'Give us five sheets will ya?'

'Five?'

'Yeah, I make a lot of cuntin' mistakes, y'know?'

'He does, the dick,' O'Toole says and nods, leaning against the doorway, hands in pockets.

'Shut you.'

O'Toole laughs. The boy laughs too. 'Sure,' he flicks five off the thick roll inside his jacket. 'It's fifty so.'

'No bother, scan. Friday arigh? Th' oul' lad will be home by then, sort me out, like.'

'That's grand, Johnny. '

In Room Twenty-Two during foundation Irish, Mann taps the boy on the shoulder.

'I see you've competitors, Brush,' he says in low tones.

'What's that?'

'The scum-boys. They're selling sheets to First Years down at the complex. Fifteen pence each. They're making offers that can't be refused, I hear.'

'Hmm. Very enterprising. If they don't sell to our year I suppose I don't give a fuck...' the boy says.

On Friday, the boy stands talking to Conway in the assembly hall cloakroom. Marley and O'Toole arrive at the door.

'Hey Brush, can you give us ten sheets there?'

'You owe me for the other sheets?'

'What other sheets?' Marley says, using a funny tone, the boy thinks. 'I didn't get any other sheets.'

119

The boy is in shock. What does he mean he did not buy any other sheets? He cannot believe someone could lie so plainly. Even in *Home and Away* the bad characters try and cover up their lies. Is it a dream, he wonders. Marley looks at him blankly. 'I want ten sheets,' he says.

The boy almost takes ten more of the roll. Give him the ten and he will go away. Conway walks to the door. 'I have to go,' he mutters.

O'Toole trips Conway and pushes him over. 'Get lost, you faggot-woman,' O'Toole growls.

'Fuck off,' Conway mutters and is gone.

'I gave ye ten last Tuesday, ye owe me fifty pence,' the boy says, spitting the words out.

'We didn't get any sheets Tuesday, did we Joe?'

'Nope,' O'Toole leans at the door, looking bored.

The boy smiles. 'Ha-ha, fuck you.'

Marley's arms are like wire, a solid centre seems to drive them, he pushes the boy against the radiator. He is shorter than the boy, but his face burns with pain.

'No, fuck you,' Marley says, shaking a little. He spits on the boy's face. The boy drops the sheets. They slide all over the floor, getting dirty. O'Toole absent-mindedly rubs his boots on some near the door. The boy pushes Marley forward. 'Let me go!'

Marley grunts and they are gone.

The boy picks up the sheets, his finger trembling wildly. He folds them into his schoolbag. Most are ruined, creased with large dirt patches at the edges from the floor tiles. His heart is not in it anymore. He tosses the few salvageable back on the

120

shelf in the art room when Mr Kirk is occupied amongst his three boxes.

Jimmy asks him for a sheet on Monday, another shiny pound coin in his hand.

'Sorry, shop's closed down. It's getting too risky,' the boy says.

English is now the only remaining subject he has to leave room twenty-two to join the honours class in room eleven. Mrs Morahan hands him back his latest assignment. The 'D' at the bottom of his composition is in red ink.

'You might consider going to pass,' she says, walking away. The idea of going to pass English is attractive. He will have to do virtually nothing. Upstairs, the syllabus Needham and company are studying is laughable. They are reading Huckleberry Finn yet again, preparing for questions such as 'Name one friend of Huckleberry Finn?'

'Sound,' the boy says, closing his book. At the next English lesson, he stays in room twenty-two for the pass class. He starts drawing another Liverpool F.C. crest while the student teacher talks about Tom Sawyer.

Outside of English, maths and Irish, everything is taught in room twenty-two. During cancellations, some of the class try to catch up on homework. The boy, Corless and Conway hang around the back of the room trying to break the lids off the desks.

'Stop making noise,' Farrell says one day, writing furiously, as the screws groan under pressure.

'Fuck you, Farrell,' the boy says. 'Ya duck,' he mutters.

121

'What did you say?' Farrell says, tossing his pen at the wall.

'I said fuck,' the boy retracts. Farrell looks mad. He leaps across the classroom, pushes the boy against the wall.

'What d'ya say, ya cunt?'

'Fuck you,' the boy says. He tackles Farrell using the 'attack is the best form of defence' technique. He rams fists at Farrell, Farrell hits back, something scrapes the boy over the eye, Farrell's lips bleed. They slide over the desks, someone is shouting, the girls are roaring.

'Stop!' Orla yells. They push and pull, the boy lands against the window, banging into the sill. They stand, breathing heavily.

Farrell's shirt is out, he wipes blood from his lip.

At four o'clock, Farrell elbows the boy at the bag shelves, the boy elbows him back. The boy does not like to scrap, he is scared at the idea of it happening, but when it is provoked, he is surprised at his bravery and he enjoys the respect it earns afterwards. He is not the weakest, he can fight Farrell. But he wishes the whole thing was over.

There are regular skirmishes now during free classes. When they collide, headlocks become a tactic Farrell uses to stop the boy's onslaught of punches. The boy can smell Farrell's sweat in the awkward hold. He becomes adept at avoiding Farrell's swinging arm.

'You're one of the best scrappers in Second Year,' O'Brien tells him one day. The boy is proud of this. Nobody else tackles him. Carvey and Needham talk on friendly terms.

Even Marley, back from another long suspension, says 'How's craic, Brush?'

'Howya Johnny,' the boy reciprocates. 'Back for another while?'

'Th' oul' lad says I have to come until I'm fifteen anyway or the filth will be onto him,' Marley laughs madly.

'John, will you go somewhere?' Peter F. Shylock says to Marley, meeting him at the end of the corridor.

At the end of the summer term another argument over noise erupts and the boy and Farrell tackle each other again. Like lovers, they know each other's soft spots, Farrell's lips burst easily, his arms are weak, the boy's nose is often exposed, he is easily winded. The scrap continues for longer than usual. The class are buzzing on the brink of long holidays, they roar encouragement.

'Beat him, Brush,' Orla shouts.

'Come on, Ducky!' Rebecca howls.

The door opens and Peter F. Shylock stands in the corridor. 'Out!' he says.

They stand in silence for a long time outside the office.

'Them fucking women, making noise,' Farrell says, eventually.

'You can't keep them quiet,' the boy agrees.

'Good ride is what they need,' Farrell says.

'Yeah, that's it,' the boy says, glad of the release of meaningless conversation.

'We'll say we were arm-wrestling,' Farrell says.

'Oh yeah. Good idea.'

'See the match the last night?' Farrell says.

'Crystal Palace? They threw it away.'

'Ye need to get a few defenders, they never got over losing Hansen last year,' Farrell says.

They wait for over an hour. It is half past three. The boy knows he will have to be released at four o'clock.

Peter F. Shylock arrives at the top of the stairs. He stares at them. Slowly he descends the steps, taking a bunch of keys from his pocket and opens the door of the office. They are going inside. The boy feels ill.

Peter F.Shylock directs them through the door with a practiced ease. The boy had almost completed two years without the official trouble-makers' seal. The floor is the only carpeted area in the building. A soft leather chair is behind a wide walnut desk. The yard is in full view of the window, the boy realises Peter F. Shylock can sit and observe the pupils every move without hindrance. Even the smokers' trees seem shockingly close.

They stand flat against the wall. Peter F. Shylock closes the door and walks around his desk. His shoes making a padding sound.

'Have you anything to say?' he says, looking out the window.

'We were arm-wrestling, sir,' Farrell says meekly.

'Arm-wrestling?' Peter F.Shylock says, turning rapidly to Farrell, moving his face even nearer than usual. His hand grips Farrell's shoulder. 'I'll put you through the wall, you bloody liar!' he says.

'It was, sir,' Farrell groans.

Peter F. Shylock looks at the boy. 'Get outside,' he says to Farrell.

Farrell walks out, shutting the door quietly. 'You are a very lucky boy, let me tell you,' Peter F. Shylock says. He puts his right hand on the boy's left shoulder. The grip is tight.

'I am well aware of your disruptive behaviour in almost every class since Christmas. I know you were behind the mindless vandalism in room twenty-two–'

'Sir, I didn't–'

'Don't interrupt me! You smashed the lids of desks, you ripped the radiator off the wall! And you were stealing sheets from the art room, oh yes, Mr Kirk has made me aware of all that. You are aware of your ability, but you do not seem to want to use it, a price you will have to pay long enough, believe me. If it were any other time of the year you would be getting two weeks suspension for this evening's performance. And that would be an indelible mark on your academic record. Now, listen to me,' Peter F. Shylock moves his face closer to the boy. The boy moves his head back, hitting the wall behind.

The grip on the boy's shoulder tightens further. It reminds the boy of the wood vices they used in art and craft in sixth class with The Master. It seems like centuries ago.

'When you come back in September, you will have a different attitude about your education, do you hear me?'

'Yes sir.'

'Yes sir, that's right. Because at the first sign of trouble you won't be getting suspended.'

Peter F. Shylock's grip tightens until his fingers seem to be in contact with the boy's shoulder bone. The pain is agonising. 'You'll be getting expelled. Now get out and tell that fool to come in here.'

III

Sonic is doing cartwheels like he is on drugs. My brother is watching Doyle play closely, but I'm fed up of it now, since we got through that cuntin' 'Jungle Zone' and those fucking levering seesaw logs, that took us eight months to figure out.

I go out to the kitchen and put the kettle on. I see the keys on the windowsill. I take them, go back to the TV room, nods at Melvin and Doyle and sure I'm the man and we head outside, me rattling the keys in me hand.

I turn the ignition and the car throbs beneath me. Smooth as butter, she idles. I'm clean now off the clutch, no more piss-artist conking, Melvin is in the dead man's seat, the two magoos are in the back, Doyle beside them. We pull out onto the road, I keep the lights dead, Agnes' oul' bitch of an oul' lady across the road wouldn't be long telling Th'oul' pair. I take off to the left. Mighty wide wheels on the Toyota Corolla, great yoke.

I rev the shit out of her as we climb the hill, swerve round, down by the school and past Doyle's house.

'Better turn on the lights,' Melvin says.

In the darkness, it is probably a good idea. I take off, putting the foot to the floor, flick the gear handle into third, fourth, roaring seventy down the road.

Motherfucker!!!

We leave the village behind, zooming up and down hills. The handy thing about driving at night is you can see if anything is coming the other way, so I take every corner pure sharp.

I'm really showing off now, driving as fast as I can, eighty, on a narrow enough road around bends, if there was a car somehow there without lights on, or some fool out

126

wandering, they'd be mowed, mowed, mowed, motherfucker. We turn off onto a rally road boreen, riddled with potholes, dips, hairpin bends, sharp ridges at the ditches. Some of the track is shit quality, muck instead of gravel, and the car bounces all over the place.

'You want to take it easy,' Fucking Doyle says. Jesus, is he getting nervous now of all people. Flashes of those ads on telly with blood and steel go through my head, but fuck it, I'm in complete control of the Corolla. Rally wheels, fuel injected engine, y'see. Powerful machine, holds like glue on the road. I come off the boreen onto a straight stretch, back on flat tar again, I take her to ninety, heading into a T junction.

'Brrrush,' I hear Melvin whisper. I've done, it, I can't stop before the line, if there was something coming, we were fucked, I lock the wheels left, the Corolla skids around, across the road, up onto the ditch, knocking over part of a stone wall.

We are still in one piece. We say nothing, get out. Melvin is quickly at the front, lifts her a bit, horse that he is, me and Doyle help, my sister looks around, my brother scratching his little head, we get her back on the road. Just a scratch along the bumper. The cold air fills my lungs, I am pumping.

We get back in, I over spin wheels as she turns, the man has shown his balls. Off down the road, maybe to the one street town, to Peter F. Shylock's precious school, 'We'll ram the gates!' I shout, 'Sign off a few wheelies!' next thing the fucking clutch goes in her. She just freewheels like a dead horse's wagon, engine ticking over, clutch pedal bouncing like a yo-yo.

'You burned her,' Doyle says.

'Did I fuck, twas Th'oul lady, she's burnt fourteen already. It was well on the way,' I says.

127

'What're you gonna do?' Doyle says, waving his flash lamp around the place, moving his green woollen cap up and down, as if these antics would somehow conjure up a mechanic with a new clutch.

A light comes in the distance.

A fucking car,' Doyle says, killing the light. The car empties of people quicker than puke. The magoos jump through a nearby gate, Doyle launches himself into a bush, Melvin has gone over a stone wall years ago. I dance around the back of the car, then kneel down. But what the fuck? I get an idea.

I walk out to the middle of the road, wave down the car. It's Vinnie Tree, the village idiot. He pulls up in his mini, hops out.

'Bit of trouble, here, hee-ya?' he huffs, walking around the car, smelling of aftershave and poxy mothballs.

'Everything alright out there, Vincent?' the wife says.

'Clutch is gone in it. The bastard.' I says. 'You wouldn't have a rope?'

'A rope? Jaysus, I wouldn't, hee-ya? I better be going,' Tree says, getting into the mini and driving off, the exhaust cracking through the night air.

'Useless bastard,' I says out loud.

'What did you do that for?' Melvin says, comically emerging from the field.

'I thought he'd pull it for us.'

'Bad move. Bad, bad move.' Doyle says, arriving. The magoos lean against the car looking anxiously around.

'Why?' I says, getting worried now. If Doyle thinks it's a bad move, it's curtains.

We start pushing the car back the road toward home. It's fairly easy to move when there's a good few pushing. My sister steers.

Less than an hour later, we get to the gate of the house. Th' oul' lad's VW Golf is already there. Bollocks.

Good Man Tree must have went straight to the local and spilt the beans just as Doyle and Melvin had predicted on the way.

Melvin and Doyle give us a last push in the drive and disappear. The other two run in the front door, and sneak down to bed. I walk around the back and peer in the kitchen window. Th'oul' lady is whinging on the rocking chair. Th'oul' lad stands at the range looking into his cup, as though he's reading tea leaves or something.

I go round the front and push in the front door, feeling like I am in some kind of crime programme. I sneak down to my bed, pull off my jeans and pull the blankets over me, my arms and legs still pulsing.

The next day, th'oul lad tackles me in the TV room. He comes in, turns off the telly.

'What has got into you?' he says.

'What?' I says.

'Driving Mummy's car around at night?' He always called th' oul' lady 'Mummy' for some reason. I think he wished we were English.

'I was…' I had no excuse.

'And you want to get your head at them lessons!' 'Lessons' he always called studying. The man was in a time warp. 'Will you do alright in the Inter?'

'Junior.'

'What's that?'

'It's called the Junior Cert now. They changed it.'

'Right. Why is that?'

'Don't know.'

'So will you do alright?'

'Don't know.' Fuck off and annoy someone else will ya? Will ya?

'You better starts coppin' on a bit now. And what the hell happened the kettle?'

'The kettle?'

'When we came back the element was burned out of it?'

The keys were well hidden after that. Not that we didn't look for them.

We sit at the back of the assembly hall. It's a study class, there's a lot of them this year. They changed round the system this year, the wankers, too much vandalism apparently, and now it's the teachers that have a classroom and we have to move, no more holing up at the radiator during the breaks. They've build a new area where half of the old tennis courts used to be and they're fucking knocking all the prefabs. I watch Packie the ancient caretaker walking along smashing each window and no one says a word and the way they use to look at me for twisting off the lid of a desk. I want a job in demolition.

Corless is raving on about Mr Bean in the park again. He loves that scene. Keeps talking about him making the tea in the hot water bottle. Corless laughs silently, you can just hear this panting of breath, after he has described what he thinks is so hilarious. I mean it is funny but yer man is going into fucking hysterics or something.

My report for Second Year was cuntish in June. Failed a rake of things. It's a load of oul' bollocks school, really. I wasn't even listening to Pete at the intro. Blah-blah-blahing about rules and regulations. Might be a car dealer or something. Buying cars looks like a handy way of making a few quid. This pissin' around with books all the time. Where's it going to get ya? Doyle reckoned he'll be a carpenter. He's fairly good at the woodwork. He showed me a dowel he made the other evening. A plus he got. He was always making go carts a course.

He's great friends now with McNulty and Ford. I don't like these fellas. I knew them like, but they weren't ever part of my crew, not like Doyle, not like Melvin. Oul' nancies really. Never allowed out at night to play football down at the village school. They wouldn't dream of taking out their parent's car. Wouldn't dream of it. I know Melvin and Doyle had kind of permission, but still it was illegal, that was the main thing. But Doyle's buddies, they're pussies.

'And...he...he...uses a credit...card...for a kn-kn...knife...' Corless whispers to me and continues laughing like a buffoon that's lost its voice.

I get a bit giddy now with all the other flatheads studiously writing away, getting ready for the Christmas exams, just me, Corless and Conway at the back. Melvin is only in a couple of days a week, too much for doing, he says, on the farm.

I make a buzzing noise and play the part of Mr Bean looking around for the fly that keeps bothering him in the park. Soon Corless and Conway are laughing and even the teacher thinks it's funny. I'm good at making people laugh, it's an awful buzz, maybe like a drug, I want more of it.

In every class now, I try to do something ridiculous, enjoying the laughter of Corless and Conway, ignoring the frowns of some of the girls. They seem even more pissed off with me than the teacher when I keep interrupting English to start sweeping the floor.

At mid-term, there is a school disco. All the flat-heads go in. Meself, Melvin, Conway and Corless loiter outside the assembly hall cloakroom. Pete looks at us sideways as he passes. Fucking discos, prancing around like a prick. We go around the school pulling dustbins out to the middle of corridors. Then I decide to try and break the door restrainers in the newly built area. Fuck all to break there, with pointed blockwork and solid doors, seems like it's vandal-proof, not like the good oul' prefabs with chipboard walls and cardboard doors. But the restrainers are a bit of a weak link. Conway and Melvin giggle watching me. I break off about ten of them before Pete sees me. Corless was meant to be keeping lookout, but probably fell asleep standing up.

'The office,' Pete booms.

I don't give a fuck. I walk up there cool as you like. What's he going to do? Shoot me?

Pete doesn't keep me waiting long. I suppose he knows I've lost any worry about being there. I have already visited his luxury boudoir.

'In,' he says.

'What are you doing here?' Pete closes the door behind him. He comes up close as usual, his stink fucking breath in me nose, his eyes like Th'oul Lady's Brussels sprouts on Christmas Day, itching to leap from his bullet head skull.

'I don't know sir,' I says.

'You come to my school, do nothing in any class, apart from disruptive behaviour and after we go to the trouble of organising a disco, you go around vandalising the new doors? I know you were responsible for the fire extinguisher incident last week.'

How the hell does he know that? That little bastard First Year Tunney. I knew he was a squealer.

'What would you suggest I do? Two weeks suspension is the regulation for damage to school property. Is there any point?'

I look at him. How are you supposed to answer questions like that? What's the point? Fucked if I know.

'You go home. I'll call your parents. They can come down here with you to discuss your options.'

Ooops! One minute I was having the craic with the lads, now Th'oul' pair are been called in. They'll not like that.

'No sir, I'm fine. I won't do it again. Sorry. Stupid, I didn't want to go to the disco. I...I was a bit bored.'

Pete pulls back a few inches, giving the good fresh air a break. 'You would want to pull your socks up. If a lot of them lads prancing around the disco had your ability they would be using it.'

Where does he get all this 'ability' nonsense? Fucked if I told him.

'Sir.' I like saying sir. Makes me feel like I'm in the army. Like some kind of commando or something. I wouldn't mind joining some elite group.

133

'Bring me in ten pounds tomorrow for the damage. Don't cross my path again.'

Where am I supposed to get ten quid?

At last break, me, Conway and Corless find Tunney at the complex doors.

'You told Pete about the fire extinguisher, ya little bastard!'

'He blamed me...' Tunney tries to run, but Corless grabs him by the shoulder.

'So you said you'd squeal...'

'P-Pete said he wouldn't tell who said it...'

'He didn't, you little moron.'

Tunney looks up at me with these big owl eyes, his lips were actually shaking. If I was The Weasel I'd probably leave him tied to the roof of the complex. That's what he deserved. Squealing was unforgivable. But I decide Tunney might come in useful at a later stage. It's how these TV shows work, you hold your debtors, they owe you. It's better than cashing in straight away.

'You owe me one, Tunney.'

'Sorry.'

'Get lost for now.'

I tell Th'oul lad we have to buy a super expensive woodwork book. Even though I am not studying woodwork he still shells out. He's not bad like that. Anything I ask for relating to school they'll pay out no problem. Want money to buy a motorbike though, or an old car to drive around the field in, no chance.

I have no interest in farming, fucking torture, that's what it is, but I get to do more now than ever, slobbering around marts and cleaning out the shed every Saturday with a scraper on the tractor. Driving the tractor around the yard was a buzz at first but I'm sick of it now, you go down there and the fumes of a foot deep of shite in the yard would knock you out. I thought I'd throw up one day.

Saturday night, I go to Mass with Th'oul lad and my grandparents on his side. They have to go every week. I don't have to go. I just want to go, to go someplace. Th'oul lad usually falls asleep in the pew. Reckons he's a bit of an atheist, I think. Wouldn't go to my confirmation, didn't believe in it. Too young to confirm your religion, he made out. I didn't care either way. Actually, I probably didn't even think about it. It seems like millions of years ago. I got twenty four quid. And what an ass I was, I gave fourteen to charity. No idea. Got some reason in me to do it.

But th' oul' lad has no interest in Mass. They love it, the grandparents. Me grandmother goes right up the front. She seems to be praying half the time anyway. Me grandfather doesn't come that much this weather. They're getting old, Th' oul' lad says about them, one night after we drop them off.

I'm eating like a horse. I always have eight ham and cheese grilled in the oven every evening at half eight after the dinner at five. I stay up late watching *Midnight Caller* and Schwarzenegger films. I love watching *Commando*. I wouldn't mind being a bounty hunter or something like Major Dutch Schaefer and being dropped in a jungle on a mission. I want to have muscles like Schwarzenegger.

The best film though is *Universal Soldier*.

'One cannot be controlled – the other cannot be stopped – Van Damme – Lungren – Universal Soldier,' is the phrase yer man voiceovers the trailer.

I keep chanting this with my hard man voice in study classes. I prance around the assembly hall.

'One cannot be controlled – the other cannot be stopped – Van Damme – Lungren – Unnn-iiivvvverrrrsal Soldier!' I roar, launching to the air.

Van Damme and Lungren have massive muscles. In *The Mirror* classified section I find an ad for a book that says with twenty minutes of special exercises a day you will have a body of pure muscle. There is a picture of a smiling man with a tiny head and a body that looks like it is about to explode.

I send off for the book *How to Build a Super Physique*. Twenty-eight days delivery, money back guarantee. I'm fierce excited when it comes in a big brown envelope. The exercises are pretty weird, things like leaning against walls, rolling a coke bottle around on the floor, standing on the seat of a chair. I nearly break me fuckin' neck the first night. But I stick at it, every day, twenty minutes.

I get used to doing them and at the end of three weeks, I trace all of the exercises into a copy and send the booklet back. I get my money returned, less postage. I continue for twelve weeks using my drawings. My sister says I seem to have built up a lot of muscle. But I get sick of the exercises when I finish the course. After exactly twelve weeks I pack it in. I tell Carvey about it and sell my drawings of the exercises to him for three quid.

In May we are meant to be preparing like fuck for the Junior Cert. I spend most of my days drawing LFC crests in my copies. I take out the books a couple of times but I've no idea.

136

I haven't paid attention in a classroom since First Year. Anything teachers say is like background noise.

'What are you going to do in the future, though?' Mrs Morahan says.

'Join the army,' I says promptly. But no, I won't join no army. I might write a 'Get Rich Quick' book.

I begin work on one but quickly get tired of it. I keep dreaming about Alannah at night. I see her in German, now she sits across the classroom from me. I'm sitting next to Agatha who spits at me when she talks. I have no notion what's going on in that class anymore. It's pure boring, all of them are flat-heads that just want to study. Why couldn't we have the quizzes we had in First Year, asking us about music and those types of things?

On the 8th June we kick off. I write whatever comes into my head. Some of the maths I have an idea about. The foundation Irish is just joining pictures to simple words. A child could do it, even though I don't think Mr Fogarty taught me a single thing over three years. Actually the exams are easy enough. I guess history dates, stuff I read when I was a kid comes in handy.

The English composition question asks for a discussion on *Tom Brown's Schooldays*. 'The episodic nature of the book is contrary to the singularity of the contemporary novel. Do you agree?' Fucked if I know. After I doodle for a while on the answer book cover, I write that a short episode can still tell a whole story, like Arthur and Ray get into loads of different scrapes, but Arthur is all the time teaching Ray the ropes of the business, whether he wants them or not. Then I write a pilot for a TV series, but I run out of time halfway through.

Science is a bit tricky and German is a complete disaster. I'm not sure how my art project will be received. I kind of got fed up with it and just fucked the mass of mutilated lemonade bottles, painted lollipop sticks and random balls of paper mache into the exam envelope early in May. Mr Kirk has never treated me the same since the sheets affair.

After the exams, Th'oul' lad gets me to do various shitty jobs. Actually he gets me to do shitty jobs all year but more so in the summer. It's not usually hard work, like, just very aggravating. He sends me over the fields to build stone walls. I'm supposed to walk along each wall and if I see any stones on the ground, I'm meant to pick them up. Of course there are, like, millions of them. And most of them are stuck in the ground, so you have to break your fucking arse to get them out.

And the bastardin' stones are freezing. But it does not matter because I don't do anything like that. I just walk up and down, thinking about girls. Sometimes it gets so bad I start looking at the sheep. I wonder if they would stand for a ride?

Nah, I don't think I could do it. Maybe if things don't improve. What if something fucking conceived then, Jesus, it'd be like fucking *V*, except instead of an alien crossed with a human, it'd be a baby that bleats and grows wool.

Still, I have a pull while I'm at the bottom of the hill, out of the kitchen sight line. I choose Alannah today, lovely golden hair, brown eyes. I often think of her getting up every morning, imagining her sleepy eyes, her night dress, her putting on her clothes, eating her breakfast. Ah, yeah.

'I don't know,' she said the day they asked her was she going out with me. 'I don't know.' Fuck it anyway.

'How did you get on?' Th'oul lad says, scratching his sock in the kitchen. Not too bad Daddeo, while I'm out doing your fucking work. Sick of this lad, now.

'Aright,' I say.

'You weren't long.'

'Ah, I have a bit of reading to do for next year.'

'Good, good,' he says. Fuck off, will ya?

I need money that is the problem. I need to raise funds to buy a car. There is no money to be had at school so school is of little interest to me. I discuss possible enterprises at length with Melvin at night as he milks. Eventually we come to the conclusion I would sell free range eggs.

The hen idea came to me from watching Melvin organise himself around the farm. He has turkeys in one barn, suck calves in another, lambs in another. I love the way he builds up cosy little pens around the weak animals. I like the warmth of the hay in the shed, the smell of nuts in the store room. I love the way Melvin did things compared to Th'oul'lad. Th'oul' lad was always in a pickle over something. He couldn't seem to get organised rightly. Barn doors awkwardly hanging off hinges and he'd never bother to fix them. One barn at the front where he keeps the nuts, he just uses one big plastic barrel. But there is all these other barrels there, and underneath the floor is built up with layers of old shite and old nuts. Then the other barns haven't been cleaned out right for years.

Melvin cleans his barns out right every night, he polishes them until they shine.

Then there is loads of old hay in the hayshed that Th'oul lad seems to have forgotten about and an old trailer, just left there, not being used. I can't understand why Th'oul lad doesn't do things like Melvin does.

Even Doyle is better organised than we are.

'We should concrete that area,' I say to Th'oul lad one day after I've finished washing the muck off the scraper.

'Where?' he says, looking around. He does seem lost sometimes, that lad.

'There in front of the shed.'

But he just hums and haws. I hear him complaining to Th'oul' lady about me later. 'Telling me to concrete places,' he says.

I just want the place like Melvin's, neat and operating well. Like why can't we get a fucking block cutter instead of that poxy hand yoke? I show it to Melvin one rare day he comes to visit.

'Look at this useless thing Th'oul Lad has!' I says.

Melvin leaps on it, slicing into the silage pit, making it work like I never could have imagined, carving out three wheelbarrows in a flash.

'It is a bit blunt,' Melvin admits.

At the mart one Saturday I buy five pullets with twenty pound I have stashed in the room. I set them up in a little hen house over the fields. This is what we should be doing all the time. Living off the land. Not buying old shit from Dunnes Stores every week, I tell th' oul' pair.

The hens take a while to lay any eggs. I feed them some grain every morning. But in March, my grandmother starts feeding them and cleaning out from them. A few weeks later, they lay a couple of eggs. I give them to Th'oul Lady. I charge her a bit more than the shops, them being free range eggs and worth more.

Th'oul Lady pays me every week. Someone says Old Mrs McCluskey down the road likes free range eggs. Melvin, I think. But I never bother going down to her. The hen enterprise makes me about twenty pound a month, that's what Th'oul Lady gives me. I never get down to the hens too much. The grandmother that feeds them. Keeps her occupied since the grandfather went to hospital, I suppose. Not that they spoke much to each other anyway, as far as I could see. If the grandfather was there, he'd be telling me I was doing it wrong anyway. I let the grandmother take a few of the eggs for free.

Then the fucking hens start disappearing. The fox, th'oul lad reckons. He says I should have fixed up the henhouse better, I get down one evening after school and place a sheet of galvanise against the opening in the wall. Next day it has fell over and there is another hen gone missing.

Eventually the whole lot of them are gone. I have managed to accumulate eighty quid over five weeks.

I spend a fair bit of time down at the grandmother's now. I like the old house, where th' oul' lad grew up. It's pretty sparse compared to our house. The grandmother sits on an old armchair at the Stanley range most of the day, pulling hairs on her chin, counting numbers 'eighteen, nineteen, twenty'. Nerves or something. She used bake a lot once. Th' oul' lad reckoned her apple tarts were unbeatable. Every day at one o'clock, she makes bacon and cabbage with a few spuds for herself and the grandfather, the odd time he's out of hospital these days. She always turns on the TV for the *Angelus* and the six o'clock news, pushing a plug into the wall. She turns it off again straight after. They go to bed then.

Usually, I stay now on a Friday night. The grandmother doesn't like being there on her own. She wakes me around eleven to bring me in a cup of tea. Then I go out and do a bit of fencing. I like it there, it's like an escape, it's like another world.

I don't even mind farming when I'm at the grandmother's place. Things move at a quieter, slower pace. Then I go back home and the house is full of babble. I feel I have to get out, to do something. There isn't enough at home and there's too much.

Years ago, the grandmother used to get me a bottle of Lucozade from the travelling shop. It would never stop at our house as we lived across the road from Agnes' place. It used call to Doyle and Melvin too. They'd have money saved every week. I'd see it when I'd be over at their places. Yer man was a small fella, the owner, with glasses and a short pencil behind his ear. He seemed to have all kinds of sweets and bars that Agnes' mother didn't have.

There was a nice shop smell in the lorry, like a whole little world. And then when he shut the back door, that world was gone again for a while. I don't care about that now. The grandmother doesn't buy me the Lucozade anymore, probably thinks I'm too big or something. It had this nice orange cellophane wrapped around the bottle.

I do a bit of painting for her too, in the bedrooms, when I'm there. I'm not a great painter, I keep marking the skirting, but I don't seem to mind doing it. The grandmother doesn't seem to be too bothered anyway, she never says anything. She just asks me how much more paint she needs. She wants me to paint the outside too, but I only power hose it. I forget to paint it. She forgets as well.

They have a lovely box hedge around the house, the grandparents. Little path running through two lawns. Very neat. Our house has got all these wild bushes and exotic trees, th' oul' lad likes sprawling plants. I can't stand them type. I love these neat lines. I trim it as it grows but after a while I forget that too.

One day, the grandfather is home and sits on the garden wall, watching me set up the hedge trimmer. He fiddles with his chestnut pipe. Then he starts on at me not to pile the lead loops together or it'll go on fire. I doubt that but I nod and spread it out anyway. Next thing he's back in the hospital. We go into to see him.

'Middlin',' he says when I ask him how he is. A great craftsman, th' oul' lad reckoned, carpenter, stonemason, whatever. I saw him when I was a kid, cocking hay at a hundred miles an hour. Now he's just shrunk in the bed.

I wonder what it would be like if the grandparents were young again, in their prime, her baking lovely apple tarts in her Stanley, him outside cocking hay with precision. No point thinking about that now.

I stay that night with the grandmother. Next day Th'oul' lad calls early.

'Dad passed away last night,' Th'oul' lad says. First time I ever heard the grandfather called 'Dad.' Him and the grandmother always call him 'Him'. But today though, the day he dies, he gets to be called 'Dad'.

He tells me grandmother.

'Lord have mercy on him,' the grandmother says. When he goes off somewhere, organising the coffin or something, I take a look in the grandfather's wardrobe. It smells of mothballs and must. I find a bundle of twenties inside one of the grandfather's jackets, must be a couple of hundred. Nice, this would buy a motor. No good to him now, is it?

I find a car for sale in the local newspaper. I convince Doyle to come with me. Doyle doesn't come up to visit much now. He has started playing gaelic in the parish team with Quirke, Farrell and O'Brien and them little bollocks, McNulty and Ford. Doyle's not great at football but he gets a go now and again. I couldn't be bothered with that shite. Training with that mad bastard Fanning? No thanks. They left me on the bench the few times I did go this year. I was on the soccer team but we were always getting hammered and I think they just gave up half way through the season.

We take the bus into the county town. I wear my wheeling-and-dealing hat.

The fella selling the car lives in a small estate on the outskirts of town.

'My name is Tom O'Dea, if he asks,' I tell Doyle.

'My fucking sister lives in one of these houses,' Doyle says, looking around.

The seller, a fella about fifty, brings us to his garage. The car is a Volkswagen Derby.

We must look no more than seventeen but I don't think yer man is all that bothered. He just keeps on about how easy it would be to turn the Derby into a Rolls-Royce.

144

'You're in great luck lads! I just put that battery in her!' Yer man rubs his hands. 'Now, a new set of tyres, a timing belt, a brake servo, a service and maybe a new set of wipers and for only a small few quid, you have a perfect car!'

I am just waiting for him to ask for my licence but he never does.

'One hundred?' I says, in a negotiating voice, even though that is the price he had advertised.

'God bless you,' yer man says. He grabs the twenties with a thick fingered fist, and disappears into the house. I lose no time getting behind the wheel and driving away.

'I can't believe he never asked you about insurance,' Doyle says.

'Let's get the fuck,' I say, excited now. I zoom out of the estate. We take off out the country road. I soon realise the Derby is a pile of shit. It is nothing to the Th'oul' lady's Corolla. The Derby's top speed seems to be forty miles an hour, but that doesn't stop Doyle telling me to slow down all the time. I turn off the road, up a boreen we don't know, to get a buzz out of it.

'Watch the bend!' Doyle says, gripping the door handle. I see him rise his arse of the seat at one stage as if getting into crash position. That fella. I don't know what's wrong with him lately.

We call to Melvin. I enjoy parking the Derby outside his house. Melvin is fairly worried someone will see it. He finishes the milking quick style, jumps in and off we go. After about an hour of buzzing around I reluctantly let the others drive. Melvin can make her talk. He zaps through the countryside, over spinning wheels.

Doyle takes control and straight away the gear handle comes out of its socket in his hands. 'What the fuck?' he says, laughing.

It's not funny. If I had done that to his car, his poxy Sigh-era, he'd have gone mental. We fiddle around with the gear handle for hours.

When we get it back in, we find we can't get the car into reverse.

It's three o'clock in the morning. Now I realise I don't know where to leave the Derby. My house is out of the question. Doyle won't have it anywhere near his and neither will Melvin.

We choose an old barn owned by a big dairy farmer, Sloane.

'He won't notice it for a few days. Sheds all over the place, that lad,' Doyle says. The empty barn is in the rallying boreen, isolated and fairly well hidden from sight. We back it in and shut the door.

It's the Friday night before I get back to the Derby. I draw pictures in a copy of my new vehicle and its logo, V W. Maybe I could do it up and sell it. I dream about re-spraying the body work, putting a big spoiler on the back, installing a stereo system. I don't bother going over to it all week. *Minder* is on, a new series. I think Ray is going to tell Arthur to fuck off.

We cycle out to yer man Sloane's place Friday night. The windscreen and the back window of the Derby have been smashed. The battery is gone. Cunts. Melvin goes for an old battery while me and Doyle clean out all the glass. We drive up and down the boreen. It's a bit tricky with no reverse and cold without front or back glass. After about half an hour of

146

driving up and down the boreen, we decide to call it off. We park it back in Sloane's shed with no real alternative.

Sunday evening, Melvin calls to tell me there is a Ford Escort dumped in a field near him, belonging to an ancient farmer who rarely leaves the house anymore. We go there and take out the windscreen and the back window. Melvin is fairly handy at this craic. They don't fit too well on the Derby, so Melvin fills the gaps with expanding foam. It looks pretty weird but at least the car is sealed. I pour in another fiver of juice from th' oul' lad's lawnmower drum.

'Let's take her for a right spin,' I say. The man has balls. Back out on the main road, full blast, foot to the floor. Motherfucker!

We pass my house at eighty miles an hour. Someone is looking out the window at the shop.

'I think Agnes seen us,' Doyle says. I swing around the corner and get back into fourth.

'McKeown is coming!' Doyle says, sounding like a girl. McKeown, the new village guard. I drop to third as I pass the school and Doyle's house, I put the foot down. I zoom past Quirke's house, the Doc is probably at the kitchen table studying his commerce book.

Motherfucker!

I'm afraid to look in the mirror to see if McKeown is still following us. I swerve up a boreen and off onto a mucky track running behind a silage slab. McKeown's fairly new, he mightn't know all the turns. Doyle leaps around the back seat, as though that will conceal him. Let's hope I don't have to reverse anywhere. A road block or dead end would be fatal now. But we seem to have lost the car, according to the eagle-eyed Doyle.

147

I get back on the main road and cruise back up through the village. Just as I pass the school again, the clutch goes in the Derby. It's the Corolla all over again! For fuck's sake! I freewheel along, the gear handle has come off in my hand.

This time, I see the car lights approaching in the mirror, passing Agnes' shop. McKeown must have caught up.

'Is it the clutch or the gearbox?' I say to Melvin as the car slows. But Melvin is gone years ago, the dead man's door swings in the night.

'No time to find out,' Doyle says, he pulls at the door handle. 'Do these doors not open?' he screams.

'Not from the inside,' I says as the Derby comes to a halt in the middle of the road. The car lights behind flash past the school.

Doyle leaps into the front.

'What's wrong with ya?' I says.

'I'm not getting arrested,' Doyle says and disappears into the darkness.

I follow him and run into the hedge. I push through the briars and clamber around barb wire nailed to thick branches. The lights of the Derby beam down the road. The car behind comes up. It slows, drives around the obstacle in the middle of the road. It's a mini. It's fucking Vinnie Tree again. Looking closely at the Derby, before speeding away. Probably straight to the local to tell everyone.

Now that the clutch is gone in the Derby and Good Man Tree has registered it and will shortly announce its mysterious presence in the middle of the village road to everyone who'll listen, the car is not long for this world. Melvin says we can dump it in their bog five miles away. The problem is getting it there. We push the Derby into a nearby field and head down to Th'oul' lad's hayshed. Melvin knows a way of starting tractors without the key. You just touch two wires together with a screwdriver near the manifold. We drive up the Massey Ferguson 35 to the Derby. We tie a rope and pull my first car to the bog. I drive the tractor, Melvin steers the Derby.

Doyle provides communication on stopping, starting and turning through the aid of his flash lamp on the back of the tractor, as unfortunately the 35 has no lights, or reflectors for that matter. After a while, he gets pissed off and joins Melvin in the Derby. We push her into a corner behind a mound of rushes.

'It'll be alright there,' Melvin says, sounding like an undertaker. Still, it was good craic. We drive back in the tractor in silence as the dawn arrives. At six in the morning I climb into bed, and sleep instantly.

With the money I've left, I send off for a book called *The Lazy Man's Way to Riches*, another one in *The Mirror*'s classifieds. I gave up reading them papers *The Guardian* and *The Times*. What do I care about Japan's economic growth? In the tabloids you get to see tits and read warped letters about cross dressers and cheating husbands, you get to read about Liverpool's possible return to glory.

The ad title reads 'Get Rich – Quick and Easy…' I am fierce excited about this book. Twenty-eight days for delivery. It promises that following the instructions will result in a sports car, endless foreign holidays, a huge mansion with a swimming pool, all the girlfriends a man could dream of. I love reading the advertisement over and over again.

I tear open the parcel when it finally comes. The 'book' is actually eight pages with a bright blue cover. There are a few sections about motivations and drawings of people drinking from champagne glasses and leaning against sports cars and a lot of pound signs. Then there is this short chapter of about two pages at the end about methods. The methods, the only methods I can see, is to put an advertisement in a paper like this fella did and get people to send twenty pound to you. Then send them on this booklet. It's a bit like the body-building book but at least that had exercises you could copy out.

There is a Money Back Guarantee. I put the book in an envelope and fuck it on back to them. The money comes back two weeks later. I'm surprised. He couldn't make much sending back the money I think. Maybe most people don't bother returning it. In fact, it's not a bad idea. But I couldn't be bothered with it. I was expecting something a bit handier then writing a fucking book.

Next thing it's time to shear the poxy sheep. Another whore's cunt of a job. I, of course have to do the hard work, because I'm a 'young lad' while Th'oul lad relaxes. I have to pull the smelly bitches out of the pen, wrestle with them until they are turned over and then drag them half a mile to Quick Tail Tom who shears them.

'A bit slow for a young fella?' Quick Tail Tom said to me grandfather last year.

'Sorry to hear that,' Quick Tail Tom says when Th'oul lad tells him my grandfather is no more. 'I would have been at it if I'd heard.'

Yeah, right, you would, you greedy bastard. I remember when the fella we used to get, years ago, was killed in an accident on the tractor. Quick Tail Tom was at the funeral shaking hands with all the farmers, telling them he sheared sheep. Oh, I didn't miss that, and I was only a slip. These fellas, they don't miss a trick.

My brother and sister are of course useless in this job, only good for jumping on the tied fleeces in the wool bags to make room. I have to pull the sheep out one by one. It's hot and flies buzz around me. There is the stink of sheep shit everywhere. My jeans are green with it and fogged with wool. Whatever you wear for the day's shearing you have to throw out after. There is a brief respite when we go inside for the dinner.

It's amazing how clean the house is when Quick Tail Tom comes. I wish it was like that all the time. Range neatly burning, kettle steaming, plates on the tables, fresh salad, lettuce, tomato, hard-boiled egg, ham, brown bread, soap at the sink in the back hall with a towel to dry your hands. If only th' oul' lady was this organised all the time.

There is a certain register to my parent's voices when Quick Tail comes in, 'How are you Tom?'

That's right, Tom, three bags full, Tom (no pun intended).

Then they'll complain about the price he charges when he fucks off. Still it's nice to get fed. I feel like a man, like a hard worker, like I deserve this food at the table, like I'm one of them tough gents now. I have a burst of energy after the dinner, even though my legs are sore and cramping. Out again, now I won't give in to the sheep, fuck you Quick Tail, keep your mouth shut, I keep delivering them faster and faster. Quick Tail Tom is one of the quickest in the county, three minutes a sheep, I time him. He starts always around the head, the wool comes off like ice cream, peeling smoothly away from the back, down then to the tail and he cleans the underside before lifting the shorn animal and tossing the fleece to one side.

Th'oul' lad pulls the lumps of green sheep shit off and then stretching out the fleece like a blanket, folds it down to about four fifths, coming to the tail-end, where he takes it and twists around until he makes a kind of rope of wool, then, holding the rope, he rolls the rest of the fleece tight, into a square parcel and pulls the rope around it twice, real tight, before looping it inside and there's your tied fleece. My grandfather, God rest him, could do it a lot neater and faster than Th'oul lad. But Th'oul' lad doesn't do a bad job, in fairness.

At one stage, I see someone walking along the road outside. I am in the zombie like state of grabbing sheep after sheep after sheep, but the flash of yellow catches my eye. Our pen is right at the main road, down from the shop. There is a thick hedge along the side. As I am struggling, I see a tossing of blonde hair and a laugh. The light honey tone. Girls. I look again as I re-enter the pen, they are nearer now, I see a face, Rebecca. And another girl. What is Rebecca doing over here, this is five miles from her house. She walks over here, for what? The other girl I don't recognise, probably a cousin. They look in through the hedge. We are too far away to say anything. But she sees me, pulling the sheep out, sees me covered in shit, smelling like a sewer pit. The expression she has is of complete disgust. Revolted. She laughs with her companion, swinging a bottle of something, tossing her sweet blonde hair. They walk past. If I was in a TV programme I would sneak off up the road, say hello to Rebecca, the friend would piss off and we would somehow end up in my bedroom, shifting. But I'm not in a TV programme. I'm in a badly built sheep pen.

I can see the end in sight now, there is only about twenty of the bastards left. It gets more difficult though to catch them when they have room. Last year, Melvin tried to explain this technique he has of knocking the ewe. See, what th'oul' lad told me to do was to grab them on the back and pull like fuck until you got to Quick Tail and then go for the underside and twist her, onto her arse. But Melvin told me to grab the snout and propel the ewe by tweaking the tail. There's only a stump as we ring them when they're lambs. Then when you get to the shearing station you just turn the snout and pull, pushing at the hip. The ewe falls over. Then just pulls her up on her quarters. It is a lot easier. But a bit more skilled. Sometimes I do it Melvin's way, sometimes when I am fed up I just do it the hard way. The hard way is easier when you're fed up to fuck.

Th'oul' lad looks a bit confused when I do it Melvin's way. He had shown me the other way, the poor bastard. But he never says anything. I get to the last one, and Th'oul lad pulls her, for luck, he says. I'm too tired to be that bothered. I just want get out of the heat, flies and sheep shit. My hands are soaking from wool grease. They say it's great for the skin, the wool grease. You wouldn't think it looking at Quick-Tail and Th'oul lad, the wrinkles on them.

It's the hardest four hours of the year. Quick Tail get his cheque, spitting on it as usual and we pull the huge wool bags into the trailer. It's over and I lie on the bed for hours, too tired to even wank.

In July we go to our first disco, me and Doyle. We get a lift from his oul' lad. Enid and Alacoque, one of her fair tasty friends from Fourth Year, are smothered in perfume and talk loudly all the way in. Doyle starts raving on about a sports car that's parked outside the hotel when we get there. It's creamy, with a massive spoiler, alloy wheels, a glass gear handle. Class. My mouth waters.

Inside the music is on full blast, I can't stand the fucking noise of it. A few of the plainish girls are not bad looking, covered in make-up. Wearing short skirts and tights. I sit near one for an hour, drinking a coke. My leg brushes against her leg at one stage. She sits quietly, looking at the dancefloor.

Doyle is talking to that wank McNulty about a Second Year woodwork project. I see one of the Fourth Years holding hands with Rebecca. Yer man has a ponytail like I had once, but a lot longer. I hear later they were locked in a spare room in the hotel for hours. Orla is there and a lot of the flat-heads in junior cert. Carvey and Needham wouldn't dream of going to something like this. I hear Carvey drinks beer in his local with the other hards every Friday night now.

In August, Th'oul lad decides to cut the hayfield. The weather will be good for a few days. I ride over with him on the Massey Ferguson 35 with the finger mower on the back. He is all go, Th'oul' lad, all professional like, oiling up his blade.

'It'll be a long day,' he says.

'How long to cut it?' I say. I can't think where I was the previous years, this must be the First Year he has brought me.

'Oh, at least four hours,' Th'oul' lad says. Four hours to cut it. And what will I do, I wonder. Wander around after him? Off he goes knocking the meadow while I stand, hands in pockets, at the stone wall.

'What are you doing?' he shouts, after he has gone about ten yards.

'Hah?' I say.

'You go ahead and look for any stones.' Ahaha. Right.

But after twenty minutes the finger mower is busted. 'Damned thing,' Th'oul lad says, getting down from the tractor.

We have to get the local fella to cut the hay with a rotary mower. He flies through it in an hour. There doesn't seem to be a need for me to walk ahead to check for stones with this guy. Why not?

Th'oul' lad hands him a cheque, he smiles at the man. When he is gone he says yer man robbed him.

Next day, he turns the hay with the tractor and hay turner. I am assigned the insanely boring job of 'shaking the hay' with the hayfork. I don't know how to do this, why I am doing it or when it is done but th' oul' lad has handed me with a hayfork and told me to 'get on with it.'

As I walk along in the sun, the tractor humming over at the other side of the wall, doing whatever it is I am supposed to be doing with this hayfork, for some reason I start thinking of your wan Agnes across the road. She is well in her twenties now. Used to babysit me for a good few years. I think she is some kind of poxy secretary this weather. I can see her watching telly through the window in the evenings, when I go over to the shop to get milk. I imagine walking through the shop in the connecting door to the house, into the sitting room.

I imagine her telling me to open my jeans and let them fall to my ankles. I have a big rod on.

She tells me to start pulling, I start pulling. I want to have a pull now. Th'oul lad has stopped the tractor. He is round the back fiddling with something. I nip over to the hedge. I get into the other field and have a good pull thinking about Agnes ordering me around

155

'Pull it,' she'd order.

Fuck yeah, fuck yeah, fuck yeah. Tits, fanny.

Th'oul Lad does not seem to notice when I leap back into the field. I feel like pure shite. I'd say I was gone to the jacks if he asks. But he's off again, turning the hay.

It's like feathers now, light as fuck. I think I'm meant to make it easier for the baling machine. We don't cock hay anymore. My grandfather was great at cocking hay. But th' oul' lad wasn't great according to himself, and I haven't a clue.

The same fella that cut it for us bales it. He is there for about two hours. It's a bit surreal after, all these weird square golden things around the cropped field. Like there is some kind of different atmosphere now. We have to stack them together in fours, they make little pyramids. The field is now like some planet on an old space programme. Th'oul' lad is moaning again with his chequebook as he waves yer man off.

Bringing home the bales is a tortuous process. Awful hard work. We have to put eighty of them on a big trailer and draw them to the hayshed. Putting them in the hayshed is like standing in a fire for an hour. The heat. I don't know how many loads there are. At the beginning I count the bales, it's so boring and hard. I make up a song I sing in my head about each number.

'Bale number sixteen, sixteen, sixteen. Six-six-six-teen, teen, teen.' Pulling the twine up, my fingers get sore. 'Twenty-seven, seven, sev-sev-sev, seven.'

'Bale number seventeen, seventeen, seventeen, la-la.' Soon I get bored of this. My arms are tired and my legs shake. We keep going grimly. I pretend I am presenting a radio show in my head.

'Pete Popse here, live from the hayfield. Any requests? Number thirty-one-one-one-thirty two, two, two, a cracking old number-ber-ber. And now let's hear Robbie Robertson with 'Somewhere down that crazy River.' …Yeah…I always see you down at Nick's café…. No. I cannot do that while I am doing this bleeding job.

Each load has to be tied down with rope. Sometimes I build, th' oul' lad draws the bales to the trailer. Other times he builds, I draw. The drawing is harder, but the building is skilly work. The first time, I made a bollocks of it and the whole load fell all over the road. Me on the back of the tractor watching. Nothing to do until the bales stop dancing all over the road. Grimly putting them back on the trailer, building again as cars waiting queued up. Doesn't take as long to build though, when the bales are at the trailer. Th'oul lad didn't give out about it. He's not bad like that. He probably did the same himself.

My grandfather was at this with us until last year. I have to do more now, being bigger an' all. The grandfather used say, 'You done well,' to me when we'd finish.

Th' oul' lad doesn't say much in the evening. 'Great to get that done,' maybe, or some shite like that. He has a can of lager, I have a bottle of coke. It's nice to sit down. My legs are still throbbing but there is great pleasure in the couch.

We watch The Paul Daniels Magic Show. I wish I had a job like Paul Daniels and doing fancy tricks with cards instead of arsin' about with hay and shite. And look at the fine bit of gear, the assistant. He married her, the jammy bastard. 'We should finish it tomorrow,' th' oul' lad says getting up.

I don't see much of Doyle or Melvin over the rest of the Summer. Melvin is usually flat out milking and only talks

157

about working all day with some farmer or other. There is fuck all craic with him, he doesn't seem to hear me when I mention possibly pooling our resources to buy another car. Doyle is painting their hayshed roof for weeks. Melvin does ridicule Doyle whenever I'm talking to him.

'Did you see the paint Hoggy was using? That's not for hay sheds at all. Fucking eejit.' Calling Doyle 'Hoggy' is a serious insult. But Melvin doesn't really care.

'I never really liked Doyle anyway,' he says, another night.

I feel sad, like, I thought we were all friends. Melvin doesn't even like Doyle. Never really liked him, he says. After all we have been through, football, breaking into old shops, the cars. And now he says he never really liked him. Maybe Doyle doesn't really like Melvin that much either. But I think it's more rivalry with Doyle.

'Did they get a new Zetor?' Doyle asks me about Melvin one night. That type of thing. Maybe because they are going to both be farmers in the village. Fuck knows.

Maybe they say stuff about me and all. Doyle tells me Melvin knows I'm in bed until noon most Saturdays because I leaves the curtains pulled. Actually I never draw back the fuckers. I don't like the light. I'm not too bothered, I don't really care. Although when I think of Melvin roaring up the road in the Zetor at half eight and laughing with some farmer about me lounging in bed and half the day gone, it gets to me a bit.

I don't know what's wrong with them. They never visit, we don't play football much. This is pure wrong, we should be together, getting on like before. I don't understand it at all.

By August, I have had enough of sitting around the house, going out doing various tortuous jobs with th'oul'lad. If I see another bag of turf I will go bananas. It's nearly all home now. I won't even go into it. Another thing that Melvin does awful fast and we seem to do painfully slow. I hate the bog, hate all the poxy insects that land on ya, hate dragging big lumps of sods from the mucus ground. Th'oul Lad seems to love it. He reckons when he was young huge families would come for the day, making bonfire, cooking sausages, telling stories and getting all the work done in no time because there were so many in each family. Of course we don't bring my siblings half the time. They're too small to do anything. The only food is a cheese sandwich. It's mostly just me and him. The grandfather used come for years. He was fast in the bog, the grandfather and he was well in his seventies. But he's dead now.

IV

It is cold at seven thirty in the morning. The boy sits in the passenger seat, looking out the glass. His father taps the steering wheel. A radio show is on, his father nods at points made by politicians. The car trailer rattles behind. They drive through the small one street town, passing the abandoned hotel, the school entrance. The avenue gates are closed, weeds have sprouted along the speed bumps during the summer months, the hedge on each side has encroached over the drive.

They cross a long bridge and pass through a small railway crossing. The mart is an assortment of multi-level galvanise roofed sheds amongst acres of pot-holed concrete outside the town. His father pulls up the black VW golf at the grey entrance booth. He gets out and a rush of cold air enters the car. His father walks over to a small wired covered hatch.

'What ring is the weanling sale in this morning?' the boy hears.

A small man blows clouds on the door of the car. The boy rolls down the window.

'Can you move her on, there?' the man says.

'He's just in the office, he'll be out in a minute,' the boy says.

'Can you just pull her up, out of the way?'

The boy shakes his head apologetically. 'Aright, aright,' the man says, shaking his head and walking away.

The noise of the sheds can be heard across the concrete. Looing, roaring of voices, the clattering of gates. His father gets in.

'Somewhere over there, it is now,' he says. His father drives the car, the car trailer rattling behind, across the bumpy surface. They walk through a door at the end of one long building. The boy waits as his father talks at a counter.

They enter the sales ring through another door, at the bottom of a tall grey wall. A man sits in a glass fronted box high up, speaking quickly.

At the sales ring, a concrete wall is topped with tubular steel. The floor is carpeted with sawdust, spots of animal excrement and stains of urine. A sour-looking man stands in the centre, in a long blue coat and wellingtons. A small Charleroi calf walks around uncertainly. The sour man prods the animal with a long piece of plastic tubing. This is the professional stick. If the boy were a proper farmer, that is they type of stick he would have, not the amateurish piece of hawthorn his father taps against the step he stands on.

The boy catches words, something like 'fort-fort-fort-fort-fort-six-forty-y-' and 'in-one-one-one-one,' but mainly it is a babbling, a stream of numbers the boy cannot understand. His father makes a sign as though to clutch something soft and sticky and lifting it from a bowl. The boy wonders where his father learned this sign. He may have made it up, but the boy doubts it. The auctioneer in the glass box notices the boy's father, nods, says something to another man beside him, lower, almost out of sight.

The boy climbs up the huge wooden steps which are actually seats, and he gets to the top, where he views the whole area. To the left of the auctioneer's box hangs a huge digital screen, containing information on the lot number, weight, animal certification. The numbers change every few minutes as each beast is led out and another led in. The boy gets a pleasure reading the information as it arrives in the bright red digits.

A huge sign over the door to the pens reads, 'Have you protected your herd? Bortex for Tapeworm.' Underneath is a photograph of a mature bullock, staring at the camera, frozen in time. Lone farmers sit on the steps in front of him, one coughs, one fills a pipe, one nods at the auctioneer, another reads a small slip of paper with clouding glasses.

Around the ring, men lean against the tubes. Some hang arms around others' shoulders, one man rubs his hand along the far side of another's torso, whispering something in the other man's ears.

His father continues bidding with less salient movement, nodding, even merely twitching his eye is enough now to notch a bid. It is important that the jobbers don't identify easily who they are bidding against. They know farmers try to buy directly from the sales ring, but they hate the practice. They will try and distract farmers at the ring, by speaking softly to them about what treasures lie in straw outside in the jobber's trailer, rubbing their arms along the farmer's side, or they will approach the farmer on the steps of the auditorium, exaggerating salutations, shaking hands, elaborating on useless weather observations. But this will only happen if the jobber does not have a serious interest in the beasts for sale at that time. Timing is everything in the sales ring. The jobber must weigh up which is more important, securing a beast, or removing the farmer's ability to buy.

His father turns and nods at the boy, the business is done. His father has six numbers written on a small piece of paper.

As they leave the sales ring, someone jabs him in the ribs.

'Howya, Brush,' it is Quirke's brother, he smiles, with an expression of pity, the boy guesses. Quirke the older wears a blue overalls with the emblem of the mart on the breast, the legs hidden underneath green plastic pull-ups over wellingtons.

'Are ye buying or selling?' Quirke's brother continues, walking with the boy out of the ring, into the sheds. Here, the multi-level roofs cover one enormous expanse of gates and penned cattle, wide aisles where red-faced farmers chase loose beasts, swinging sticks of pipe and hawthorn. The noise is deafening. The boy's father hurries ahead down the aisle.

'Getting a few weanlings,' the boy shouts.

'They're pricey enough today,' Quirke's brother yells.

'Are you working here long?' the boy says.

'Every Saturday morning the last few years,' Quirke's brother nods, with an air of long and tired experience. 'On yer feet all day. But a few quid anyway.' Then Quirke's brother is gone, the conversation over, the boy is cold again, he looks for his father, now at the far end of the aisle looking up and down at the sheet of numbers in his hand. The father sees the boy, and beckons him with impatience.

'Where did you go?' his father says. 'Here, take these numbers and start looking for them.' The father tears the bottom three numbers off and hands them to the boy. The boy walks around the pens, looking for 801, 817 and 334. There is no order to the numbers in the pens, every grouping have random figures. Cattle loo and spit, drool drips from their large mouths. The calves are squashed against the gates in some pens. There is a strong smell of beef, dung and urine.

He finds 456, 876, 120, 001, 987, 876, but there is no sign of 334, 801 or 817. His father comes along prodding three beasts.

'These are half of them,' he says. 'Did you not get any at all?' The boy says nothing, holding the paper at arm's length, as though it burns his fingers.

'Jesus,' his father says.

'Watch them fuckers,' a man says, from behind. Two more weanlings brush past his father and join their three.

'Fuck them anyway,' the man behind says, a wide face under a short brimmed hat.

'Come, come, hup, hup!' the man says, whacking all five beasts in turn.

'Easy,' the father says, 'this pen is empty, we'll get your two out of it.'

The father guides the five into the pens. As one weanling dashes off the aisle, he jets soft steaming excrement across the concrete. The boy steps over it carefully, a strong hot smell running up his nostrils.

His father runs around the beasts as the other man shuts the gate.

'Pure fucking wired,' the man says. The beast loo, the noise rings in the boy's ears. He stands in his wellingtons, which allow the hardness of the concrete to come through, the rubber has no soft sole to protect the feet. His father dives between his three weanlings.

'Let them out, let them out,' he roars to the boy.

'Pull the fucking bolt, wake up, will ya,' the man says beside him. 'Slow for a young lad, hah?' the man says to the father, who grunts, as he prods one of the beasts.

'Go over the far end,' his father says, when the wide-faced man and his two weanlings are finally gone. 'You might find them over there. I'll try this side again. Maybe they hadn't been penned straight away.'

More blue-overalled staff walk along a narrow raised platform between the pens. One notices the boy looking over each gate. He has a large ginger beard with curly hair past his shoulders. He wears sunglasses. He walks up to the boy at the end of the platform.

'Are ya alright there, what are you looking for?' the ginger man says. The boy shows him the numbers.

'Why didn't ye tell me? I'll get these for ya in a minute. I know where everything is. Sure ye're meant to give us the tickets.'

Within a few minutes the ginger man has the three weanlings in the aisle. He moves the cattle with a practised ease, gently directing them with light prods of his tube of piping. 'Where do you want them?' the ginger man says.

'We're over there. See the man with the beard.'

'Ah yeah. Grand.'

His father reverses his trailer into a gate directed by the ginger man. The ginger man quickly unbolts the back door and smoothly drives the cattle in. His father smiles.

'Thanks a million, Gary.'

'No bother, no bother,' the ginger man nods, returning to the maze of pens.

'Good. Let's get going,' his father says.

In the distance, through the thin lower branches of the beeches, the yellow bus comes up the avenue. It jolts over the speed bumps. The engine roars as it turns in toward the entrance porch, the windows are fogged up, the driver scowls at the autumn air outside. It comes to a stop behind the Ford Granada. The girls at the front get off.

From the sixth row back, the pupils remain seated. Mad-dog looks in his rear-view mirror.

'Come on to fuck!' he says.

'Stick!' Quirke the older says. He sits in the middle of the back seat.

'Come on!' Mad-dog says.

'Stick, stick, stick!' A few of the Leaving Certs chant along the back seat. The boy sits in the outside of the second seat from the end, looking up the aisle.

'Stick, stick, stick!'

Mad-dog thumps the steering wheel. He gets up slowly, walks down the aisle.

'Ooohhh…' the students hiss.

'What's this shit about Quirke, ing?' Mad-dog says to The Daddy.

'What's wrong Jack?'

'Are we going somewhere?' O'Brien says. There is a burst of laughter.

'I had enough of this last year with ye, ing. If ye lot keep doing this there will be trouble. Now get off my bus!'

'Oh, yeah, we're getting off,' The Daddy says.

Mad dog shakes his head, walks back up the aisle.

'Stick, stick, stick!'

A First Year looks back and gets up, swinging his schoolbag around his shoulder.

'Where is that little Lally kid off to?' Quirke the younger says.

'Moffat, tell that little prick to come down here,' Quirke the older says.

A Second Year runs up the aisle. 'The Daddy wants you,' he whispers to Lally.

The First Year follows Moffat to the back seat.

'What's your name?' The Daddy says.

'James Lally.'

'Where the fuck were you going there?'

'I was… I was getting off the bus.'

'Did you not hear us shouting stick? Do you know what stick means?'

'Eh?'

'Come on!' Mad-dog roars.

'Stick means you don't get off the fucking bus until I say so, do you know that?'

'Oh. I don't want to get into trouble. Sorry. '

'Come on!' Mad-dog howls, his face beetroot. Lally turns up the aisle.

'Where are you off to?' Moffat grabs him by the shoulder and shoves him back.

'Cheeky bastard!' The Daddy says. 'You First Years have it too good anymore. When I was starting we were put face first into the fucking toilet bowl, did you know that? After they'd pissed in it. '

'Oh,' Lally says.

'Oh? Oh what? Do you know who I am?'

'No.'

'He's your Daddy now,' Quirke the younger says, smiling.

'Oh.'

'Oh what?' Quirke the older says.

'Come on Jesus Christ, for the love of God!' Mad-dog whines.

'Oh…Daddy.'

'See this bag. You have to carry it around for me anymore, do you hear me?'

'Yes, Daddy.'

Quirke the older throws the schoolbag into the First Year's chest. He grabs it. His eyes are moist.

'Come on, let's go,' Quirke the older says.

'You should call him fag,' the boy says.

'What the fuck is that?' O'Brien says.

'Fag like in *Tom Brown's Schooldays*. When the seniors had servants, the First Years, they called them fags.'

'Tom what's what?' Conway says.

'I'm going in to get the Principal, if that's what ye want?' Mad-dog shouts.

'He's rubbing his chest,' Quirke the younger says. 'Better not push it, Damo.'

'Alright,' Quirke the older says. 'He'll probably have a heart attack. Let's go. Come on, fag, move!' The Daddy pushes Lally up the aisle.

'We'll stick for half an hour tomorrow, Mad-dog,' Quirke the older shouts as he gets off the bus.

'Ing!'

Peter F. Shylock speaks at the top of the assembly hall. The boy stands on the right, in the second last line with the Fourth Years. His hair dangles around his shoulders. The first bristles of a moustache sprout above his lips. He pushes his hands in his pockets, a small orange cloth bag around his shoulder. Within, there is a pencil case and one copy, a lunchbox and a bottle of coke.

'I want to draw your attention to the school rules and regulations as outlined in the school homework diary. In particular, smoking is forbidden anywhere in the school, on the school grounds or coming to and from the school in uniform, either on Bus Eireann services or by foot. Strict consequences will result in anyone breaking these rules. Last year, we introduced the teacher-classroom system and it has been very successful. You will receive a timetable today and as with last year, you will move to the specific classroom for each class...'

Carvey tries to wrestle the ball from the boy. The boy evades him, using the desk as a barrier. He launches the ball forward, Mann catches it and runs past Needham, around Mr Fogarty's desk.

'Touchdown!' Mann roars.

'Can ye put those desks back where they were, like good lads and we will get on with the lesson,' Mr Fogarty is saying.

'That's fifteen to ten,' Mann says.

'Is it fuck,' Needham says. 'That one Brush got didn't count.'

'Why not?' the boy says.

'Because you took it before the time out was over.'

'Ye had no time outs left!'

'Will ye take out your books and we will look at the exercise on page twenty-five,' Mr Fogarty is saying.

'Hey Brush, are you going to the disco Friday night?' Agatha says, flossing her teeth at the windowsill. Her brace glints in the sunlight. Beside her, a ginger-haired girl is buttering cream crackers with pickle.

'I...don't know,' the boy says.

'Should come, Brush, they're good craic,' Agatha says.

'Noel, can you take out your book, like a good man,' Mr Fogarty says, catching Needham's elbow with a two-fingered grip.

'What are you on about?' Needham says to Mr Fogarty, shaking off the teacher's thin fingers. 'Sure I got a fucking A in the Junior.'

'It was only joining dots in fairness, Needles,' Carvey says, walking up the classroom

toward the door.

'Fuck you, Carvey. An 'A' is an 'A'. You're a great teacher, Tommy. Keep up the good work.'

'How do you get your hair so shiny, sir?' Agatha says. 'Do you use, like, brylcreem or vegetable oil?'

'Would you put the ball away and make a start on these exercises,' Mr Fogarty says, walking up to the blackboard.

'It's actually an American football T,' Needham says. 'Hey, Carvey go, go! Make a run!'

'We're not ready,' the boy shouts. 'Mann, mark Carvey, quick!'

'Go!' Needham throws the ball as the boy dives on him. Mann jumps toward Carvey who reaches for the ball. Carvey catches it.

The classroom door opens. Peter F. Shylock stands outside, open-mouthed.

'Touchdown!' roars Carvey, his face breaks into a wide smile, his back to the door. 'Fucking great fucking catch, motherfuckin' bastard, although I do say so myself!'

'The problem is…,' Conway says, chewing crisps on the bus. He sits on the edge of the third row back, facing the back seat. 'that classroom-for-each-teacher craic means Pete is always watching Fogarty's room now.'

'How long is Carvey gone down for?' Quirke the younger says from behind.

'Three weeks,' Conway says. 'Not bad for playing American Football during Irish.'

'He'd want to watch it or he'll get gate,' Farrell says, perched in front of the back row, where Quirke the older and two other Leaving Certs pass around cigarettes.

'And Pete didn't say anything to ye?' O'Brien says.

'No, sure we were sitting down by the time Carvey got out of his way. I think he was so obsessed with Carvey, he wouldn't have noticed if we were smoking,' Conway says.

'Good oul' craic though,' the boy says. 'I don't know how ye lot stick that honours Irish.'

'Have to, Brush,' Farrell says. 'Th' oul' pair would go fucking mad if I went down to pass, never mind foundation.'

In the complex at lunch time, the Fourth Years find a large blue weight which they try to deliver to life over their head. Carvey and Melvin can lift it quite comfortably. Needham cannot lift it. Mann lifts it after a long struggle. As he holds it aloft he freezes.

'And now I can't get it down,' Mann says.

Quirke, Farrell and O Brien cannot be encouraged to try. The boy eventually lifts it.

The competition advances to attempting to lift the weight a number of times. Melvin lifts it five times, Carvey ten, then Melvin lifts it ten. Carvey lifts it twelve, then Melvin fifteen.

The boy lifts it six times to murmurs of praise.

Conway cannot lift the weight at all. Jimmy Moran won't attempt to lift it, while Joseph Moran arrives and lifts it twenty times.

Ryan tries to lift it when he and his crew are summoned by a First Year fag. All of the First Years are referred to now as fags, since the boy introduced the term. When Keadin hears the record is twenty, he lifts the weight twenty five times. There is some disquiet among Carvey and Melvin that they had already lifted it a number of times between intervals.

Doyle and some inter certs arrive at the large crowd now milling around the blue weight. Doyle cannot lift it.

Doyle and the inter certs go to the woods and dig up large rocks which they start lifting over their heads. A technique becomes popular of holding the rock over the shoulders and when letting go, walking out before the rock comes down. One boy that does this does not walk out quickly enough and is knocked unconscious. An ambulance is called.

Peter F. Shylock calls Assembly the next morning. 'Lifting objects in the complex or large stones unearthed in the woods is not permitted. A pupil is in hospital today with a skull fracture due to these unauthorised activities.'

When they are as explicitly declared as illegal as smoking, the lifting games become more popular. Ryan runs a book on the blue weight. The boy reaches eight. Keadin refuses to lift it again, complaining of his back. Carvey scores forty, Joseph Moran fifty, Melvin fifty-one, after which he sits down for a long time. Some of the competition winners do not attend school for the rest of the week. Melvin has pulled muscles. Carvey has to take time off from the butter factory. The boy has sore arms for some nights. Packie collects all the rocks in a wheelbarrow and disposes of them. Miss Tuohy has the blue weight and other heavy objects removed from the complex.

The boy meets Doyle at the shop. He does not wear his green woollen cap anymore, he is dressed in a denim jacket and jeans.

'How are you getting on with Alacoque?' Doyle says.

'Fine bit of gear,' the boy says.

'Doesn't want to do the Leaving this year, Enid says.'

The boy sits later in his bedroom, alone, watching the television.

'How do you like being back in Fourth Year?' the boy says aloud.

'Handy enough being in Fourth Year, you'd have done all the classes before?'

'You going to the disco Friday night?'

'Do you and Enid always go to the same discos?'

'That Fogarty is an awful fool, isn't he?'

'Did you perm your hair? Enid was saying you did…uh.'

The boy stands with Mann and Carvey at the top of the stairs.

'You should send off for it,' the boy says to Mann. 'I'll give you a few of the exercises, if you want. You still doing them, Gerry?'

'No. I get enough exercise in the butter factory,' Carvey says.

'Yeah, but these are targeted to build up the biceps, y'see,' the boy says to Mann.

Alacoque comes up the stairs. Her black hair shines from the light through the window. Her fingers hold a bundle of text books, exercise books, a pink transparent pencil case. Her perfume can be sensed as she arrives on the landing.

'Is Mrs Morahan in today, do you know?' Alacoque says, looking directly at the boy, her eyes focussed.

'Don't know,' the boy mutters, turning from her, walking nearer Carvey. 'It's a great fucking book, though.'

The boy is in religion class. His desk is attached to the seat, and he drives it like a vehicle around the room in circles while the student teacher chases him. Alacoque looks back as he does it. She smiles. When the teacher finally reaches him, he opens the window and climbs out to the car park. He comes

174

back into the classroom a few minutes later as the teacher is putting the desk back in place.

'This is not funny, I am trying to teach a class. You should have more sense,' the teacher says.

The boy smiles at her, gets back behind the desk and begins driving around the classroom. After a few minutes, he parks in the corner where he sleeps.

Through many classes now he sleeps. He puts his hands on the desk and pushes his head in between, closing his eyes. Teachers do not interrupt his sleeping.

During the religion class, the door opens. Peter F. Shylock gestures to the boy.

Needham nods obediently and reaches across, tapping the boy on the arm.

'What the fuck?' the boy says, sitting up. He looks at Peter F. Shylock and gets up slowly. He walks out of the class and follows Peter F. Shylock to the office. The sun beams on the carpet, the room is warm.

'It is only the first week of October and already numerous reports are coming in about your behaviour,' Peter F. Shylock says, standing very close to the boy. 'Constantly disrupting classes. Organising dangerous sports around the complex.'

'Sir, that wasn't...'

'Intimidating First Years on the bus...'

'What, sir...'

'Shut it. Why don't you just clear off?'

The boy looks at The Principal. Peter F. Shylock walks around the walnut desk and returns to stare at the boy.

'We have a small number of very troublesome pupils at this school. Some of them come from highly dysfunctional backgrounds. I have met your family. This is not the case with you. Some of these troublesome pupils are of limited intellect. Despite my reservations and your appalling academic record here, this is not the case with you. Some of them have psychological issues. Some of them just don't want to be here. Why are you here? If this is the road you want to travel on then, so be it. I have done all I can. There are other courses available for youths in your category. You would be better off in one of those than here. I advise you to think about that. Now get out.'

The boy is handed a note by Mac on his way out of the school on a Friday evening.

'You have been suspended from the school and all related school activities as of the above date until further notice. Please present this note to your parents who I would ask to arrange a meeting at my office by telephone with The Secretary as soon as possible. Regards, Peter F. Shylock, Principal.'

The boy lies in bed on Monday morning. Mad-dog's bus pulls up outside, the engine idles for ten seconds, then it revs away, carrying his sister.

He gets up at eleven, makes scrambled egg and listens to The Pat Kenny Show. He starts making a newspaper but after a few minutes, scribbles over the front page, tears it out, puts it in the range. He lies on the couch in the TV room and watches cartoons.

'A few ewes to dose this evening,' the father says, looking in, holding a small bottle of worm drench.

'Grand,' the boy says. 'Bollocks,' he whispers.

His mother is at work. At three his brother comes home from primary school. His father cooks dinner. At quarter to five his sister comes in from school. When the mother comes home, the boy and his father go in the Volkswagen Golf and dose twenty ewes. When they return an hour later, the boy goes to the kitchen, eats a dinner of sausages, beans, potatoes and returns to the couch in the TV room. He watches *Minder*, but changes the channels often during the programme. He watches the news, a quiz show, a gangster film. He stays up until five in the morning watching a western and a documentary about sex change patients.

He masturbates twice before going to bed.

On Saturday, the boy and his father are fencing. The father uses a crowbar to bore holes and drive new stakes in gaps. The boy swings a billhook, a curved blade on a long handle, to hack a bush into a space. They pull a line of barbed wire along the field boundaries. The boy strains the wire at thick hawthorn trunks with the claws of a hammer, taps in the staples, curved fencing nails, with a flat stone.

They carry the role of barbed wire around, its weight bending them at the start of the day, lightening as they use it. They attach an extra line of barbed wire to the tops of field boundaries. The boy knocks down the branches of hawthorn into gaps,

They drive to the shed in the VW Golf at three o'clock. The boy drives the tractor, pushing deep layers of animal excrement off the floor around the cattle into a deep pit at the side. In the evening, as darkness comes, the boy fills two bags of turf at the shed by his grandmother's house.

They drive home. At the back door the father says 'I don't know what you'll do. There is nothing for you here.'

It is Thursday before Peter F. Shylock can see his parents.

They come through the entrance doors, walking along the new recreation hall, where part of the yard and tennis courts once were, past the assembly hall cloakroom, along the old corridor and to the left to Peter F. Shylock's office.

They knock, The Principal opens the door.

'Thank you for coming down.' He has arranged three chairs in front of the desk for the visit.

They sit, the boy in between his parents. Peter F. Shylock sits behind the desk.

'Your son has no interest in participating here any longer. I don't want to expel him. I would rather he left of his own accord. But his position here is becoming untenable.'

There is a silence of half a minute. Peter F. Shylock looks across the desk at the boy's parents, his eyes reaching one, resting there, and then moving across to the other.

'Where do you think he should go?' the boy's father says.

'There are some good new Youthcraft facilities now operating in the county. Forgive me for speaking bluntly, but I think it is something you would appreciate. They specialise in taking on difficult cases. Your son has expended his privileges at this school. I am sure I can refer him to some local centres.

'But what do they learn there?' the mother says.

'A variety of trade basics. Carpentry, Metalwork, Car Mechanics. It's like a preparation for an apprenticeship.'

'I'm not sure if he's cut out for that sort of work, are you?' The mother looks at her son, who stares out the window. 'Is there no hope of him staying here?'

'I'm afraid your son will clarify that. He has made his position clear, have you not?' Peter F. Shylock looks at the boy.

'I wanted to join the army,' the boy says quietly.

'The army, but…,' the father says.

'The army. Yes,' Peter F. Shylock says. 'Where particularly high levels of discipline, punctuality and concentration, not to mention a tight haircut, are essential. I would shelve that one. Look, I really can't spend any more time on career guidance. We have over four hundred other pupils at this school, most of whom want to be here. I believe I have given you the best option available?'

'Yes, yes thank you,' the father stands up.

'It was nice to meet you again,' Peter F. Shylock says. They crowd at the door. The Principal reaches in amongst them and turns the handle. The parents and the boy file into the hall.

'So… is he out?' the mother says.

'What?'

'Is he out of the school?'

'I told you I am not expelling him if I can avoid it. I presume he is officially withdrawing, is that right?' Peter F. Shylock says to the boy, nodding his head slowly.

'No,' the boy says.

'Eh?' Peter F. Shylock stands up straight, looking at the boy closely.

'I think…I'll want to stay in the school…for the moment,' the boy says.

'But we have just discussed how little interest you have, and how a trade preparation course would be more appropriate. This is part of the problem,' The Principal eyes both parents alternately. 'His attention is very poor.'

'I'd say…I'll improve here,' the boy says.

'Would that be possible? If he worked hard?' the mother says.

Peter F. Shylock looks at his watch. He pulls the office door closed behind him and locks it with a key.

'You can send him in on Monday while you consider his options. Now, I really must get on.'

The boy sits quietly in the classroom during foundation Irish as Needham and Carvey wrestle on the floor. He draws LFC crests on his exercise books.

In the yard, he walks around with Melvin and Conway, listening to their conversation. Sometimes he walks up the hill, past the tennis courts, to the trees. Murphy does not come out of the school at lunchtime anymore. He is usually in the recreation area reading a biology book. The boy walks through the dead leaves, looking up at the bare branches, lifting in the breeze. He shivers. Two First Years stand at a tree trunk, talking and counting conkers. He looks at them for a moment and walks down the hill, to the complex door, where Melvin and Conway shelter from the draught at the side of the building.

The boy sends twenty pounds in a postal order to one of the adverts in *The Mirror*. A booklet arrives twenty-eight days later, titled *How to Score with Women*. There is a drawing of a smiling women, holding a triangle shaped glass on the cover.

He reads the pages closely. The text emphasises the female evaluation of the male's eyes as a method for gauging his attractiveness. It outlines the need for conversation in the process of achieving physical gratification.

'The female requires a 'give and take' dialogue. However, she will respond in abundance once precisely targeted questions are posed. Particular queries known for success are those which relate to the female's clothing, leisure pursuits and family. Work or school are inadvisable fields as they tend to instigate undesirable combatative type emotion. It is important to always veer on the side of caution and never criticise any aspect of the female's clothing, leisure pursuits or family regardless of their opinion on same. A key strategy is to take a keen interest in the female's leisure pursuits. For example, if the female has a known interest in stamp collecting then the pursuer should immediately attain an encyclopedic knowledge of the stamp collecting industry. Conversation will then flow more easily. It is important to note that the ratio of talk should be ten-to-ninety in favour of the female. Yet the ten percent must present someone of intelligence, backbone and humour. The key is to never to present fear, but to exude tenderness.'

The boy reads the booklet repeatedly, every night. He underlines passages, circles diagrams. At the end there are suggestions for dates.

'Walks are cheap and good for holding hands. Activities such as these lead to ease of access to the next stage, which will be outlined in the follow-up text, *How to Sleep with Women* (Only available to subscribers to this book).'

The boy stands at the door of Mrs Morahan's classroom, the old room twenty-two, waiting for the teacher. Alacoque walks in the corridor talking to another girl. The boy waits for her to come near. He watches her, looking at her eyes. She does not look at him. She drifts past, standing at the door, still talking to her friend.

Kevin Arnold on *The Wonder Years* plucked up the courage to ring Winnie on a recent episode. The boy watches the programme now every Thursday evening. Winnie and Kevin are a couple, they go to the cinema, they go to a milkshake restaurant, they 'make out'.

Rebecca and a boy with a ponytail from Leaving Cert are announced as a couple in November by Orla during a study class in the assembly hall. They walk up the new recreation area holding hands. The boy watches Rebecca's boyfriend, inspecting his head from afar, thin brown hair tied back, his face narrowing downwards to an abnormally pointed chin. The boy examines himself later in the mirror. He spends longer brushing his hair, checking the strays above his lips.

The boy does not study German in Fourth Year. He attends woodwork in the new workshop built where the art room was demolished. He only sees Alannah in the yard at break time. He cannot sit near her anymore.

'Who is Alannah going out with?' the boy says casually to Ryan at the complex doors.

'He was at the last disco. Sitting on his knees all night, she was,' Ryan says. Keegan digs his hands deeper in his pockets, against his crotch.

'Were you there, Rob?' the boy says.

'Keegan doesn't go to discos.' Keadin says. 'Too busy up the mountain, eh, Rob?'

'Ah, slack oul' craic, that,' Keegan says.

When the boy's licence comes through, he decides to drive to the Sale of Work. Doyle arrives at the boy's house dressed in his denim jacket and jeans. He wears a black leather studded band around his wrist.

'You're ready for action, I see,' the boy says.

'Handy if there's any hassle,' Doyle says, checking the band.

The event is as it was two years earlier, a few of the studious pupils helping out around pensioners and teachers at tables of cakes, buns and attic rubbish. The boy drives out the avenue back into the town.

Marley and O'Toole stand near a phone box in the town square. They salute the boy, who pulls the tractor up.

'Ho scan,' Marley says, as he walks over to the tractor.

'How craic,' O'Toole says, sitting on a wall. The boy gets out.

'What are ye at?' the boy says.

'This and that.'

'Good yoke, is it?' O'Toole says.

'Does the job,' the boy says.

'Gets you from A to B anyway, scan,' Marley says.

'Or A to A-and-a-half,' O'Toole says and laughs. Doyle has got off the tractor and walks around, twisting his studded band.

'I'd say we'd want to be heading home,' he says.

'Hurry home are you, Doyler?' Marley says, taking out a comb and brushing a fringe of curls.

'I like the comb,' Doyle says and smiles.

'Do ya?' Marley says. 'What do ya like about it?'

'What? Oh, nothing.' Doyle's smile fades.

'No, what do ya like about it, Doyler? Huh, scan?' Marley smiles to O'Toole who rolls a cigarette, sitting on the wall. Doyle stands near the telephone box.

'Come here, I'll show ye a trick. Have you change for the phone?' O'Toole says to Doyle.

Doyle takes out a twenty pence piece.

'I'll give it back to ya in a minute,' O'Toole says. 'Watch this.'

O'Toole takes the coin and goes into the booth. He puts his hands around the telephone casing. He looks underneath, runs the twenty pence coin along the side. He moves closer to the telephone as though hugging it. Marley moves to the left of the booth.

'What are you at?' Doyle says. The boy sits on the front wheel of the tractor, looks around the square.

'He has a way of using the telephone box as a cash machine, d'ya know?' Marley says. 'Look at this bollocks.'

Marley points at O'Toole, still with his back to them.

'Look, he has it, the jammy bastard! Look over there, Doyler!' Marley says, jumping, pointing at the telephone casing. Doyle moves to the door of the booth, trying to see over Marley's shoulder. Marley steps around Doyle and takes the booth door. He swings it backwards, pushing Doyle tight against the perspex. O'Toole turns around and smacks the perspex. Doyle howls in pain.

'Hey lads, fucking hell,' the boy, says coming over.

'Problem, Brush?' Marley looks up, still holding the door. O'Toole smacks the Perspex again. Doyle's studded

184

band comes off and falls to the ground. His groans are muffled.

'Get the fuck,' Marley says.

Marley lets go of the door. O'Toole comes out of the booth and flings the twenty pence piece at Doyle. They jump over the wall.

'Wankers,' Doyle mutters, panting. His nose bleeds.

At the weekend before the Christmas Exams, the boy takes out the books from the shelf in his bedroom and leafs through them.

'Going to continue on, are you?' the boy's father says from the hall.

'I suppose. Might as well.'

'Do your best anyway, sure, that's all you can do,' the father says.

The boy reads the history book from cover to cover one night. He looks at the old black and white photographs of army leaders. He reads the commerce book, 'goods of merchantable quality' he mutters under his breath. Using a ledger he draws up a profit and loss account of his financial situation. He finds a surplus of seven pounds and forty eight pence. At the pocket money rate of five pounds a week he calculates he will be a millionaire in three thousand, eight hundred and forty six years.

The Christmas report is a marginal improvement. The boy has only failed French.

'Maybe you could turn it around,' his father says.

He does not know any French, he explains to his mother. A teacher of French lives nearby, the mother arranges grinds.

Every Sunday, the boy cycles to the woman. They spend three hours doing French verbs, compositions, comprehension in her small sitting room where an open fire blazes. The teacher gives him apple tart and cream afterwards. He enjoys the weekly apple tart and cream and the open fire. He does not improve in French class.

The boy and Doyle arrange a day's mitching with Enid. He deserts his sister on the road before the bus arrives. He finds Doyle and Enid crouched underneath a wall near their house. They wait until Doyle's parents go away for the day.

Doyle's house is much older than the boy's, wainscoting on the walls, ribbed glass panels in the doors. Enid cooks scrambled egg and beans at one o'clock. They watch *Grange Hill* on the TV. They drive Doyle's father's old Ford Cortina around the yard. Doyle puts on his denims and buys sweets in the shop.

'Agnes' oul' lady was doing awful looking at me,' Doyle says, cycling into the yard.

A few days later the boy mitches again, this time on his own. He sneaks around to his window and taps on the glass. His brother opens up.

'Give me a jumper there, and my black jacket,' the boy says, pulling off the school top. 'And my E.T. Wallet.'

The boy hitches a lift outside Doyle's house. An old woman picks him up and brings him to the county town. He explains he has to go to the dentist. He wanders aimlessly along the paths. The morning rush peters out, the streets become quiet. He goes into a barber shop.

'Short back and sides,' the boy says.

'Are you sure?' the barber says. 'You want all this hair off?'

'Yeap.'

His neck is cold afterwards. He walks up and down the main street. He buys *The Mirror*. He sits in a coffee shop and orders coffee and a jam doughnut. He stares at the models. He goes to the toilet with the paper. He masturbates. He wipes himself with toilet paper. He comes out and finishes the coffee. He walks around the town. He goes into the church. He blesses himself with holy water from a fountain at the entrance. There are three old people at the top of the pew. He sits at the back. He kneels. He gets up and sits on the pew for a long time.

He walks to the lake at the outskirts of the town. He watches the water drift by. The lake is deep. He walks along the edge, tossing little pebbles in.

The Parish club are holding a dinner dance.

Farrell sells the boy a ticket at school.

'Don't go getting pissed at it now, Brush,' Farrell says.

The dance is at a hotel in the county town. The boy wears a purple woollen jumper and a pair of blue jeans. Melvin's father brings him and Melvin in.

'What age are you now?' Melvin's father says.

'Sixteen,' the boy says.

'Don't go drinking tonight, ye bitches,' Melvin's father says.

Doyle arrives with McNulty and Ford. They sit together at the other end of a long table.

'Are you getting a pint?' Melvin says.

'I don't know, are you?'

'Might,' Melvin says. Melvin buys a pint of lager. The boy buys a pint of Guinness.

'Remember it's not how much you drink tonight, but how much you shite tomorrow,' a fat man says at the bar.

'This is horrible,' Melvin says, at the table. 'I'd rather drink fucking coke.'

After the meal, a man plays records in the corner. Groups of older men and women sit around talking. The boy sits beside Melvin, listening to the conversation.

The boy drinks the pint of Guinness very slowly. He finishes it as the anthem is being played. Farrell and Melvin have four pints each.

'I thought you said it was horrible,' the boy says to Melvin, as they leave.

'Got better!' Melvin grins.

They go home with Farrell's father. Farrell and Melvin laugh a lot in the back seat. The boy sits at the window. A purple rash has appeared on his face, Melvin tells him.

He looks at it in the mirror in the bathroom when he gets home. It is gone in the morning.

The Leaving Certs gather in the yard during lunch. The boy is nearly as tall as most of them. He stands with Mann, Conway and Melvin at the doors to the new recreation area. Quirke the older comes out.

'Pete's gone for lunch. Think he'll be gone most of the day,' Bendy shouts to The Daddy, his eyes red.

'Calls his oul' lad Pete, the weirdo,' Conway says.

'It's all that glue he is sniffing, sure he's the whole time at it,' the boy says.

The Daddy nods. He lifts his hand. From a group of First Years at the complex doors, Lally emerges and hurries across the yard, carrying a lunchbox and bottle of orange. When he reaches Quirke the older, he pulls a rope from his pocket and hands it to The Daddy. The other end is already tied to Lally's belt.

'I bet there isn't a day goes by that kid doesn't regret his big mouth.'

'It's easy on him,' Mann says. 'I heard they used beat the First Years with hurleys once.'

The Daddy leads Lally up the stairs and into the tennis courts. He stops in the centre of some leaving certs.

'Drink!' The Daddy says.

Lally runs up with the bottle of the orange. The Daddy swigs from the bottle. He hands it to Lally.

'Sandwich!' The Daddy roars.

'Fucking bananas,' Conway says. 'I think the power has gone to his head, though.'

'I thought Doc said he was keeping quiet for the leaving,' the boy says.

'Must be the pressure,' Mann says.

'Hey, hey,' Mac says as he opens the new recreation area door, looking at two Second Years in a head lock. Mac stands and leafs through his blue folder. The Daddy has

189

dropped the rope, Lally gathers it up. The Daddy casually walks down the steps and strolls toward the complex. Lally follows behind, carrying the lunchbox and bottle of orange.

'Close one. He could get gate for that, tying a rope around a lad,' Conway says.

'Hmm. Lally won't have to put up with it for much longer, there's only a few months left,' Mann says.

'Three months is a long time for the little bastard,' the boy says.

In March, Mann organises a night out in the county town. The lift is supplied by Mann's mother going in and Melvin's father coming out.

'If anyone offers you drugs in here, don't say fuck off,' Mann says, as they walk to the hotel entrance, where the Parish team dinner dance was held. 'Just say no.'

The fat man sits at the bar. 'Not ye again,' he says.

Mann and the boy have three pints of Guinness together.

'Good arse,' Mann says, as he farts on the stool. The disco adjoins the hotel. Within the boy has three more pints of Guinness. He hugs Mann, ruffles his fingers through Melvin's hair. He jumps around on the dancefloor. He drink two glasses of green liquid. He laughs in the car on the way home.

When he wakes in the morning, he rushes to the bathroom and urinates for a long time. He goes to the kitchen and drinks two glasses of orange diluted with water. He cycles to the shed and starts filling the wheelbarrow with silage. The weanlings low loudly. The boy vomits over the barrow.

'You'd want to watch what you are doing at night,' his father says, in the evening.

'We know you have permission to go to town, Mulligan,' Marley says, standing over a First Year.

'I don't have anything. My mam feeds me at home,' Mulligan says.

'You got chips yesterday, I saw ya,' Marley says.

'Just give us the pound, you little prick,' O'Toole says, leaning against the windowsill.

They look around as the boy comes along the corridor. 'Pete's on his way,' the boy says.

'Get lost,' Marley says to Mulligan, who runs toward the end of the corridor.

'We'll be talking to ya,' O'Toole shouts.

Marley and O'Toole walk into the classroom followed by the boy. As they sit down, Peter F. Shylock passes by in the corridor, looking in through the windows along the top of the wall.

Mr Fogarty hands out sheets to the class. 'Are these shopping lists, Tommy?' Needham says.

'Shopping lists? No, these are your exercises for today. Would you get back into your seat, Noel, like a good lad. And put down that bottle, please.'

'But there is shopping things on them?' Needham says, lying down lengthways over two desks.

'How's the car going, sir? D'ya get her up to ninety, yet?' Mann says.

'Will you leave Mr Foggy alone, I'm asking him something? Do you want to confuse the poor bastard,' Needham says.

'Easy do that,' Conway says.

'Yeah, what are all the tomatoes, potatoes and shite for?' Carvey says.

'I will have to call The Principal if you don't get down off that desk,' Mr Fogarty says, biting his lower lip, flattening his shiny black hair. He shuffles the remaining sheets of paper at the teacher's table.

'Uuuuhhhh!' the class chant.

'No need to be like that, Foggy,' Needham says, sitting on a chair.

'Now like good lads, will ye behave? Let us all look at question one…Cheannaigh…'

'Ye alright for fags?' Ryan says, looking around the classroom.

'Give me two of them dirty things,' Carvey says. 'Fucking Manager hasn't paid me yet.'

Ryan tosses two cigarettes across, they roll on Carvey's desk.

'Cheannaigh? What is it? Anyone? Can you put away the milk carton for a few minutes, good lad? Where is your copy?'

'Copies, sir?' Needham says. 'We need copies? Oh, bollocks, sir, this is…'

The door opens. Peter F. Shylock leans in. The class is silent. Needham studies a sheet on his desk. Carvey's fingers close around the two cigarettes in his hand. Ryan slowly slips the red box under his jumper.

'Carvey,' Peter F. Shylock says.

'Me, sir?' Carvey says.

'Office.'

Carvey stands up, sliding the cigarettes under the lid of the desk.

'You needn't bother putting your tobacco away. Sorry about the interruption, Mr Fogarty,' Peter F. Shylock says.

'That's fine, Principal. Thank you.' Mr Fogarty says, still shuffling papers.

Carvey walks out. Peter F. Shylock closes the door. He looks at the class through the windows as he walks to the end of the corridor.

'That's him fucked now,' Needham says. The class noise grows again. 'He's only back a fucking week.'

'He'll deffo get gate this time,' Mann says.

'He better hope the butter factory will take him on full-time,' Conway says, nodding.

'Ryan, it's your fault, what the fuck are you throwing fags around the classroom for? Jesus!' Needham says.

'My fault?' Ryan says, turning around. 'Nobody is complaining when I provide low cost fags. He asked for them.'

'Them oul' Winfield, sure they are full of fibreglass, pure poison. I don't know how anyone smokes them,' Needham says, getting up and walking along the back wall.

'Could we make a start on question 1… Cheannaigh…,' Mr Fogarty says, desperately.

'That's why you bought two off me last week, is it?'

'I was stuck.'

'Exactly. I am here to fill the demand.'

'You brought them out in the open, don't you fucking know Pete watches this room all the time. You are one thick prick,' Needham says.

'You want to make something of this, go ahead,' Ryan says.

'Maybe I fucking do,' Needham takes a T-square from under a desk and swings it at Ryan. Ryan jumps up, backing against the wall.

'You better be prepared to use that, you long cunt!'

'Oh, I'll use it.' Needham lunges at Ryan.

'Please let's not have any more old messing, good lads,' Mr Fogarty squeezes his eyelids close together.

Needham swings the T-square toward Ryan's midriff. Ryan blocks it with his arm, it hits his elbow. Ryan grabs Needham's shoulder, swings him around, pushes him to the window, cracks his forehead against Needham's nose.

Mann gets up. Keegan stands and puts his arm in front of Mann. 'Stay out of it,' Keegan hisses.

Needham's nose flows with blood.

'You'll – You'll be sorry for this, Ryan.' Needham slides to the floor, blood reaching his collar.

'Don't accuse me of getting your girlfriend caught. He had his fucking paw out,' Ryan says, trembling, his face red. He walks back to his seat, rubbing his arm. He sits down and looks at the sheet in front to him. 'And he still owes me a quid for them fags.'

A girl brings a handkerchief to Needham.

'Cheannaigh? Cheannaigh? Has anyone got this one?'
Mr Fogarty says, weakly.

'Looks like Pete was aiming to nail someone.' Marley
says to O'Toole. 'Thanks for the heads up, there.' Marley nods
at the boy.

'Nice one, Brush,' O'Toole says.

'Carvey got gate,' Needham says, massaging his nose, as they
walk toward the entrance hall at four o'clock. 'He was only
back a week from a suspension. Pete told him he had no
choice, catching him with fags in his hand during a class.'

'What'll he do now, go to a school in town?' the boy
says.

'No, he'll probably forget it. I might do the same.
Bullshit in here anyway.'

'Everyone seems to be leaving except me. Houston and
Corless got ahead of the game,' the boy says.

'And Melvin.'

'Melvin?'

'He told me he was getting out for good. He's taking
over th' oul' lad's farm. Ha-ha! I thought he was your mate?'

'Yeah. But he never said…'

'Hey Brush,' Marley says, coming up to the queue
from the new recreation area. 'You at home tonight?'

'I am yeah, why?' Marley pulls the boy by the
shoulder, out of the queue.

'I have to get on the bus, Mad-dog won't wait,' the boy
says.

'He'll wait,' Marley says. 'We might have something on tonight. Would you be aright to give us a hand? Few quid involved?'

'Suppose, what is it?'

'Small bit of work. Piece of piss. Handy few pound. Around nine aright?'

'But do you know where I live?'

'Oh, I'll find ya. Don't worry.'

The horn beeps at five minutes to nine outside the boy's house. He is standing at the gable, looking at the stars emerging in the fading blue sky. The car ticks over smoothly. The boy gets in, it is a three-door Honda Civic, two years old.

'Ho craic, Brush,' Marley says, at the wheel. Furry dice hang from the rear view mirror. There is a smell of cigarettes amongst a cherry oak air freshener.

'Scan,' O' Toole says from behind.

Marley drives fast, changing gear aggressively.

The boy looks back, there are a pile of folders on the floor. On the dashboard, there is a copy of *The Irish Catholic* folded neatly.

'Nice wagon. This yer father's?' the boy says.

Marley and O'Toole laugh. 'Got the loan of it,' Marley says.

The trees tower over the car along the side of the road in the night light. 'Goin' in next week?' Marley says.

'I tol' Th'oul Lady we had no classes left. Said there was no point goin' in for the last few days.'

'Yeah, we're doing the same. Goin' back next year?'

'Don't know in the fuck.'

Marley drives down the town streets, beeping at groups of youths in corners. He turns left at an alley just wide enough for the car. They come out in a car park at the centre of a small shopping centre.

'What are we at?' the boy says.

'Nothing much. Just want you to do something, I'll tell you in a minute.'

The car comes to a stop. Marley looks around. They are at the front entrance of a large clothes store. 'You can drive, can't you?'

'Yeah,' the boy says.

'Good. There'll be a few quid in this.'

'Right,' the boy says.

Marley opens his door and gets out.

The boy goes for the door handle. 'No,' Marley says. 'You stay here. If anyone comes, blow the horn and start the car. Sit in the driver's seat. We won't be long.'

O'Toole gets out after Marley and shuts the door.

They open the boot. Marley and O'Toole take a pinch bar and a sledge out. They leave the boot open. They put on balaclavas and run across to the store entrance. They look around. O'Toole swings the pinch bar at the glass doors. An alarm rings inside. Marley hits the glass with the sledge. It breaks into thousands of pieces. Marley kicks the pane in, it falls as one fractured sheet. They run in. The boy looks around the carpark.

A minute later, O'Toole runs out, carrying a box of ladies stockings. He tosses them in the boot and shuts it. He comes around to the driver's door, opens it.

'What, all this for a few tights?' the boy says.

'Back in a minute, scan, be ready,' O'Toole says, closing the door and banging the roof. O'Toole runs into the shop. The boy sits into the driver's seat, gripping the steering wheel. He reaches for the ignition, there are no keys. He pulls the door handle. The door is locked. The keys hang from the door lock outside.

'What the fuck?' the boy says.

He clicks the electric window switch uselessly. He tries to push the glass down.

'Motherfucker,' the boy says. Marley and O'Toole emerge carrying a small safe. O'Toole waves at the boy, as they hurry to the car park entrance. The boy kicks at the driver's door.

On the street, Marley and O'Toole put the safe on the path. Marley signals, a car starts, lights flash, the car pulls up. Marley and O'Toole get in the back with the safe. The car drives off.

'Fucking bastards,' the boy says.

The boy jumps into the back. A blue light flashes. A Garda car drives into the car park. The boy pulls down the back of the seat, the panel to the boot will not come away. 'Bollocks,' the boy says. He slides into the footwell, resigned.

The garda car comes to a stop. There are footsteps, the sound of a garda radio clicking on and off. 'This is the Civic that was taken an hour ago. They can't be far.'

'Is that the fucking keys in the door of it? They must be kids.'

The door handle of the car is lifted. 'Fuck, they're still inside the shop, go, go!'

Footsteps move away from the car.

The boy looks into the car park. The squad car ticks over, lights shining across the shop entrance. He kicks the back left side glass. After three kicks it splinters. He kicks it through.

'Hey,' a voice from the shop roars.

'Hey, hey!'

The boy pulls his jacket over his head, dives through the glass, fragments pierce through his jacket, he falls to the ground, pushes his body forward off the tarmac, rolling over himself, running on to the wall of the car park. He gets onto the street, runs, turning at the first alley, there are footsteps behind him. He jumps over a wall, runs through a back garden, around a set of swings, a small inflated child's pool.

'He's gone into the Black Hall estate!'

The boy runs along the side of the house, out onto a wide road, across green areas, through another small garden, past a gable, over a tall back wall, through an alley, and turns right to behind a restaurant. There is a large bin against a wall to the left, he lifts the lid, dives into rotting vegetables, pulls the lid down. Footsteps pass along a street nearby, a radio buzzes, the noises fade, moving further away.

The boy and Doyle stand outside Doyle's house hitching a lift. The summer light is strong at seven o'clock.

'Should be someone coming along soon,' Doyle says. 'There's always someone passing.' They kick a ball up and down the road.

'Here, long one, Doyler,' the boy says, kicking it high into the air. Doyle catches it and kicks it back.

'Car coming,' the boy says.

'Oh look, this is Dominic now. He'll bring us,' Doyle says.

'He won't go anywhere anymore,' Dominic says, as he drives quickly toward the county town. He has a small white van. 'They don't know what to do with him at all. He won't go anywhere only out to milk the cows. Mam and dad are ripping that he left school.'

Dominic drops them near the cinema. They are half an hour early for the film. They go into the chip shop. The boy has chips. Doyle has a chicken burger.

'I got a great deal there,' Doyle says. 'The chicken burger is one twenty and the chips are eighty p. But with the school special you get both for one eighty. I told him I was a student and if I didn't bother with the chips, could I get the chicken burger for a pound. He wasn't too keen first but I told him it was the same thing.'

'Oh yeah?'

'Yeah, I managed to talk him into it. I'm great at negotiating things. Getting deals.' Doyle finishes the burger, rolls the wrapper up and throws it into the bin at the wall. 'What are you going doing for your woodwork project next year?'

'I don't know in the fuck. I hope I don't have to go back at all.'

'What'll you do?'

'I don't know. I can't stand much more of that place. Maybe one those Youth trade places or whatever they're called.

'Yeah? Are they not a bit rough?

'What do you mean?'

'Like they're all from fucked-up homes.'

'I don't know, couldn't be any worse. Might go to England. Or do a machine course like Dommo.'

'Right. At least those two scum-pricks won't be back in September.'

'Marley and O'Toole? Why that?'

'Yeap. They were caught carrying a safe out of a hardware shop. They'd locked some First Year inside the car they'd lifted. They've been sent to a place in Glenlough. Some type of borstal, I heard.'

'Great. That's the place for them cunts. Yeah, everyone is leaving as far as I can see. Mann reckons he'll jack too. Corless is making a fortune delivering bread, he's out every night on the beer. And I've to do the poxy Leaving. You're in for a pure doss in Fourth Year, Doyler.'

'Th'oul Lad collected my rocking chair yesterday, he met Pete down there. Pete reckoned I should be a joiner. He used be a woodwork teacher, you know. Never seen joints as well-made, he tol' Th'oul Lad.'

'Yeah? Fair play.'

'Ah, I was always fairly handy at the woodwork.'

Some girls sit in front of Doyle and the boy during the film. The girl sitting on the outside has long blonde hair. Doyle tosses winegum wrappers at her. She looks around, glares at the boy.

'Stop doing that you moron,' the boy whispers. 'She thinks it's me.'

'Arrah!' Doyle says. Doyle gets up to go to the toilet and hits against the blonde girl's elbow as he passes.

'Oh, sorry, sorry,' he mutters casually.

'What an ass!' the blonde girl whispers as Doyle leaves the theatre. When Doyle returns to his seat, the blonde girl gets up with the girl beside her and they walk down the steps. The boy stands.

'I'll show ya,' the boy says.

When he gets to the foyer, the girls are in the toilets. He walks around, looking at posters of new films. The sweet shop has closed. He walks out to the glass entrance doors. He stands on the steps looking to the path. He returns inside, walks toward the theatre entrance. An old woman sits behind the counter in the ticket box.

'How are you, love?' the old woman says.

'Howya.'

'The film any good?'

'Not too bad.'

'Out for the night are you?'

'Yeah, for a while anyway.'

'Good lad. Enjoy it.'

'Thanks.'

The blonde girl comes out of the toilet with her friend. The boy stares at her. She glances at him and says something to her friend as they walk back into the theatre, giggling. The boy walks in after them.

'How'd that go?' Doyle says, as the boy sits down.

'Tight bitch,' the boy says.

After the film, they walk to the main street to a telephone box. The boy's father answers. 'I'll see ye in half an hour, I'm just doing something,' he says. 'Outside the cinema at eleven o' clock, okay?'

They walk down the main street. The boy turns right, passing a busy line of pubs. Doyle looks around. 'A lot in town tonight, Jays. We better get back, your oul' lad'll be there,' Doyle says.

A taxi pulls up in front of them, a Mercedes E class. 'We get a taxi back to the cinema for the craic? Won't cost much. I'll pay,' the boy says.

'Aright,' Doyle says. The taxi-driver gets out and hurries into a pub. The engine idles. 'Oh, he must have a fare.'

'Might be just gettin' fags. Come on,' the boy says. Doyle looks at the pub, nods, and gets in the back seat. The boy runs around to the driver's door, sits in. The seat is leather. He puts the car aggressively into gear and drives off, over spinning the front wheels.

'What the fuck?' Doyle says.

The boy drives to the end of the street, swings left at a junction, blows the horn, switches on the hazard lights, turns the radio up to the maximum. He swerves left, drives through a car park, onto another street and leads off a slipway onto the ring road.

'Go, go, motherfucker!' he roars.

'What the fuck are you doin'?' Doyle says.

'See the sand quarry–,'

'What are you on about?' Doyle says. 'You better stop and let me out anyway.'

'See the sand quarry up there? Marley reckons they leave the keys of the artics hanging in the office, we take a swing in, huh?' the boy says.

'Will you let me out, will ya?' Doyle says.

'What the fuck is wrong with ya?' the boy says. He picks up speed on the straight, at sixty miles per hour, he spins the steering wheel right, pulls the handbrake, the car rotates on the road, a warning noise sound comes from the dash. A bus approaching behind swerves to avoid the car.

'See that, that's a lot bigger than any that fucking Melvin ever made,' the boy says.

'Are you gone mad?' Doyle says.

'Let's go, let's go,' the boy says, over-spinning the car forward. He changes gear as the car straightens up, pushing the accelerator to the mat underneath. The dial reaches ninety. 'We'd fly through the entrance gate like this.'

'Ah, fucking hell,' Doyle says, rubbing the back of his head.

The boy turns the car up the narrow quarry road. The dial is at seventy as he hits the quarry gates. They burst open, part of the front bumper gets caught in the gate and breaks off.

'Pure paper,' the boy says. 'There's the office. We'll bust the window and get the keys, take one of the trucks out for a spin. Did you ever drive an eighteen-wheeler? Marley reckoned he did this before.'

The car comes to a stop near a dispatch office at the centre of a large concrete base. Doyle opens the door. 'Where the fuck are you going?' the boy says.

'You do what you want, but I'm getting out of here,' Doyle says.

'Fuck you, why?'

'This is madness, you'll get locked up for it!'

'Why, sure we won't get caught?' The boy gets out.

'Good luck,' Doyle walks away.

'Come back here, ya cunt,' the boy says.

He runs around to Doyle, grabs by the shoulders. 'Let me go, fuck off.' Doyle says.

'Fucking Hoggat, ya,' the boy says.

The boy punches Doyle in the face repeatedly, his fist smacking against the jawbone, eye socket, cheekbone, lips, teeth. He kicks Doyle in the chest, in the ribs. Doyle tries to beat the boy away with small fists.

'Uh, ya bastard,' Doyle says. Blood drips from the top of his head as he runs off. The boy stands breathing heavily. He turns and runs to the door of the office. He kicks the window. After a number of blows, it cracks, a large piece falls in. He reaches inside, turns the latch. Inside he finds a bunch of gate keys hanging. He looks around the office. He kicks at a drawer. He walks out, sits into the Mercedes. He takes a tissue from a packet on the dash, wipes the steering wheel, the gear handle. The siren of a squad car blares on the ring road. The blue lights flash in the sky. He gets out of the car, runs to a tall wire fence. He climbs over it, landing on a pile of sand, he slides down the side, sinking into it, grains fill his clothes, his hair, his eyes.

V

Running, his feet barely touching the ground, Tunney arrives at the complex, panting, eyes red from the air.

He stops beside the boy. 'They're up there telling First Years to pay security...'

'Cheeky bastards,' Mann says. 'They'd still be in Glenlough if his oul' lad didn't know the judge.'

'They all stick together them law fellas,' Conway says.

'What do you mean?' the boy says.

'Jake Marley's a hot shot lawyer,' Conway says.

'Big practice in town,' Mann says.

'I though he stole a load of money?' the boy says.

'Some fraud thing, yeah. But he got out of it,' Mann says.

'But why does the son hang around with the likes of O'Toole?' the boy says.

'Don't know. Why does anyone hang around with anyone?'

'He reckons he's in charge now. That's what he told all the First Years,' Tunney cautiously pulls a box of Benson and Hedges through his fly.

'Still, if they put a foot wrong they'll be fucked back. It won't take them long, I'd say,' Conway says.

'Where are they right now?' the boy says.

'Up at the assembly cloakroom,' Tunney says, lighting a cigarette, shielding it with the chest of his jumper. 'Doubt they'll be in too often. Just to rough up the kids. Bendy reckons Pete's gone mad about it, but he can't do a thing...'

'Let's go up there now,' the boy says. Mann and Conway follow him into the new recreation area.

First Years hurry along, looking up at the boy towering over them. As he walks up the new stairs, he nods at a junior cert at the handrail. The student slides a steel T-square from a side pocket of his schoolbag and passes it to the boy.

At the assembly hall cloakroom, Marley and O'Toole, wearing tracksuits, are leaning against the doorway. They stand over a First Year.

'Fifty pence? What do you think we are? Where's the rest?'

'Give Dad his money,' O'Toole says.

Marley looks across as the boy nears with Mann and Conway. 'Howye lads! Got lucky, that time, eh, Brush? Good buzz though?'

The boy swings the T-Square down onto Marley's shoulder, Marley groans, goes to his knees, O'Toole jumps forward, the boy shoots the T-square deep into O'Toole's face, it cracks against the front teeth, blood spills, O'Toole falls back on the ground.

'You're dead, Brush,' Marley whispers.

'What ya say?' the boy sinks his boot into Marley's stomach. 'You're finished school. Scan.' The boy tosses the T-Square on the tiles. He looks at the First Year. 'Tell Pete they were screwing ya for security money. Tell him they started fighting between themselves over the split.'

'S-squeal?' the First Year says.

'Yeah. We'll overlook it this time. This cunt was mistaken, y'see. I'm The Daddy now. You pay me. Tunney will collect,' the boy says. The First Year nods. There is a hush down the corridor.

'We better get going,' Mann says.

They walk quickly through the new recreation area, down the stairs, past the new staff room, out into the yard, up to the tennis courts and join the kick about.

Things are different in the world. Melvin, Needham, Carvey, Corless, Houston, Ryan, Keegan, Joseph the stone-faced twin gone. Quirke, Farrell, O'Brien, Murphy, Keadin in honours classes. Even Jimmy Moran has knuckled down, wants to be a banker, the wanker. Murphy is going to be an accountant for fuck's sake. Only Conway and Mann remain in my crew at the pass classes. Even the dog-women are studying now to get a D in foundation Irish. I draw circles on my copy.

In the evening Farrell sits beside Quirke three seats from the back row. I sit alone in the back seat.

'I'm The Daddy now,' I say. Conway sits back in the seat in front of me. 'Where is everybody, for fuck's sake?'

'There aren't the numbers anymore,' Conway says, looking back. 'This route is hanging on by a thread. We'll probably end up in a minibus the way things are going.'

A sheet, passed around the class as Mrs Morahan talks to them about options, options, options, nomination for Head Boy and Head Girl the sheet reads, or nominate yourself, he writes his name in the box, Mann tells him a lot will vote for him, why not, Pete will go mad, mad, mad, that's the idea, drive them all mad, mad, mad, now get out of this get it away I want to put my head on the desk nestled in between my elbows and sleep the world away…

Peter F. Shylock comes to the former room thirteen during maths with Mr O'Leary.

'Sorry, Mr O'Leary. Can I borrow one of your pupils?'

Peter F. Shylock stands in front of the walnut desk in his office. 'Why on Earth would you put your name forward for Head Boy?'

'I don't know, sir.'

'Have you forgotten your record at this school since you came here? What were you thinking?'

'I don't know, sir.'

Peter F. Shylock stands close to the boy. 'You have been a consistent trouble-maker, vandal, bully and a perennial despicable influence on other pupils since you took your place here.'

'Sir, I haven't bullied—'

'I have given you many options to take other courses. All of your associates are now gone, they are in more suitable forms of occupation. Yet you are here and now you decide you want to be Head Boy?'

'Not really, sir. I just put it in for a joke…'

Peter F. Shylock breathes out.

Keadin is voted Head Boy. He has put on more weight but his acne is gone. He gets a kiss on the cheek from Orla, the head girl at the announcement in the assembly hall.

The boy walks around the yard with Conway.

'…great place, altogether,' Conway is saying.

'What is?' the boy says looking around the yard.

'Kind of a training centre. I wouldn't mind leaving here and going to it. You do welding, mechanics, carpentry.

Whatever you want. They take anyone. And you get a few pound as well.'

'You mean the Youthcraft centre?' The boy says.

'If Th' oul' Pair would let me, I'd be gone in the morning. Sure what is the Leaving Cert anyway, no use to you.'

'No, waste of fucking time,' the boy says.

'Look at Melvin now, milking away, as happy as Larry,' Conway says. 'And Carvey is supposed to making a fortune with the overtime at the butter factory. He's in the pub every night.'

The Leaving Certs queue up to see the Career Guidance Counsellor. She sits in a small office, piles of folders balance on her desk. 'Now what are we going to do with you?' She smiles. 'You're doing all pass subjects but you have a lot of ability, The Principal says. What do you want to do after you leave here?'

The boy scratches his earlobe.

'If you would consider third level, you would be sending off to the CAO for a college place in February. I have university brochures here, would you like to browse the courses on offer?'

'I want to do barman,' the boy says.

'Barman? Right. Have you considered any formal training? There are a lot of good courses in the hospitality industry. I think CERT offer a one-year bar tendering course in the RTC.'

'I'm not going to college.'

'You're not? But even with a reasonable pass leaving, you probably could get a place on an arts degree?'

'I'm not going to college.'

'Your parents told me last year they would be keen to see you get a third level qualification.'

'I am not going to college.'

'What about a tech college, then? Art and design?

'I want to join the army.'

'The army?' The Guidance Counsellor swallows. 'Right, very well. I don't have any of the forms here for the Defence Forces today. I'll have them posted out to you so you can look through their brochures, okay? Can you tell the next boy, eh, Mr Conway, to come in?'

The package from the Defence Forces arrives a week later. The boy looks through the leaflets at the kitchen table. Zeal, punctuality and initiative will result in promotion. Recruits are paid from day one. Accommodation, meals and uniforms are provided. He enjoys reading the brochures repeatedly. He calculates if he was promoted every year, he would be at the rank of Adjutant-General in twenty-one years. He writes his name on the form and puts it in a drawer in his bedroom.

The boy walks along the corridor, the First Years salute him, 'Daddy', 'Daddy', 'Daddy'. they say, there is a sense of power but it is not what he expected, not what he imagined. Near the office a Second Year empties a bin on the floor.

'Good work,' the boy says. Another Second Year pulls the fire hose from the wall and turns it on, water flows. The boy leans against the wall, watching.

'Pete,' someone shouts. The Second Years run toward the stairs leading to the assembly hall. Peter F. Shylock comes around the corner. 'You!' Peter F. Shylock says.

'It was nothing to do with me,' the boy says quietly. Peter F. Shylock looks at the tissues, wrappers, plastic bags, bottles, banana skins floating in a growing pool of water.

'You!' He roars at the Second Years, now at the assembly hall cloakroom. Peter F. Shylock lunges forward and slides to the floor.

There is a scream from somewhere. Peter F. Shylock turns clutching his chest, his face is a darker purple than usual, his suit is soaked.

'Hey, hey,' Mac says, coming around the corner. He puts his blue folder on the windowsill. A Fourth Year girl comes up to the principal. Mac and the girl drag Peter F. Shylock in the door of Mr O'Leary's classroom. They settle The Principal on a chair. His eyes are glazed, his jacket drips.

An ambulance comes. Peter F. Shylock has had a heart attack.

Thursday evening. The wheels of the bus go round and round. Flashes through puddles. It's only half full when it leaves the school. Area is dwindling in population, must be. At least Rebecca is still here. Something to look at. Not much else. Where is everyone? Conway not even in today. Don't know where Mann is. Long day wandering around the school. Didn't go to many classes. Strolled the corridors, I like it when they're quiet. Met Pete, seems recovered. He didn't seem to care what I was doing. Just looked at me and back at the ground as he walked past. Happy enough I wasn't doing anything wrong, I suppose. Couldn't be bothered breaking anything. Not like the good oul' days when Needham and Carvey were here. In room twenty-two, pass maths, breaking desk lids. Good craic. Nothing like that now. Feel old, feel heavy. Old orange bag has my lunch; bread and butter sandwich, roughneck flash with cold tea. Pencil case, one Othello text book. No copies even. Don't know where they are. Don't care. Only ten people left on the bus as it comes to my house.

'See ya, Jack,' I says to Mad-dog as I get off.

'Ing,' I hear behind me. Awful dickhead, that lad. Door panels shuts. Air is cool.

I have decided. I feel light. I cycle over to Melvin later. He says he will do it in the morning.

We talk for hours about cars. He brings me into his back kitchen around nine. His mother is sound, she gives me treacle cake, ham sandwiches, tea. Melvin pours a drop of Jim Beam into my tea with plenty of sugar. We do this often now. Fucking lovely. I am as happy as fuck cycling home. Next morning, I get up at seven, go in to Th'oul Lady.

'I've a pain in me stomach,' I says.

'Another day?' Th'oul Lad mutters in the bed.

'Sure if he has a pain he cannot go,' Th'oul Lady says.

'Aright, aright,' Th'oul Lad says, turning over in the bed, sighing or something. Hate the fucking smell of sleep in there.

Melvin arrives at eleven. We cross over to the shop. Melvin goes into the telephone box. I watch him slide the twenty p into the slot and put the black handset to his ear. He listens for a long time on the phone. Agnes is behind the counter this morning. Not bad looking, really. I walk around in a circle outside, something turning in me stomach.

Melvin comes out. 'He was telling me you had great potential and could have done well in the Leaving. He wished you well.'

'He thought you were me aright?' I say.

'Oh, yeah, no bother there.'

'Grand job, I'm out so!' I say. I offer my hand to Melvin, who shakes it.

'Nice work, Mel,' I say. 'Comin' over for a cup of tea?'

'I have to dose calves,' Melvin says getting on his bike.

'Finished school,' I say at the door of the kitchen.

'What?' Th'oul Lady says.

'Pete's told me I can't come back. I just rang him there. "Washing his hands of me," he said.' Good believable phrase that. 'Can't be having any hassle now, he reckons, what with the ticker playing up and all that, I suppose.' Very convincing.

'But why were you ringing him?' Th'oul Lad says.

'Just – to get an exam number. We were getting them today. Doesn't matter now.'

'He's expelled you, you mean?' Th'oul Lad says, standing up from the table. 'I don't know what to say to you. I have to go and do the herding.'

The boy stands outside Doyle's house. A car comes, he puts his hand out, his thumb pointing upwards.

'Hello,' the woman says. The boy admires the dash, the dials, the fascia, the digital display of the radio. He notices the woman has a skirt on, tights. She taps her finger on the

214

steering wheel. The boy's erection is obvious under his jeans. He adjusts his penis covertly through his pocket.

'Have you finished school?'

'Yeah, I finished last year, Mary.'

'Very good. And what do you hope to do now?'

'I'm going in to the Youthcraft place for an interview.'

'An interview? Good man, the best of luck with it.'

She would rip open her blouse as they rocked and he would suck on her tits, mouthing the mounds of 'soft fleshy milk-secreting glands in sexually mature human females' as they are defined in the dictionary, he looked it up once.

'Give it to me …fuck me…' she would say, biting his ear.

'Busy at the bank, these days?' he says.

'Oh busy enough. It's hard to know how busy we'll be any day. I'm just a cashier, so it's not like I've an appointment book,' Mary says, turning her head to him for a second, smiling. Blue eyes. Fuck, yeah. His erection stiffens further.

She used to be bank manager Th'oul' Lady said one time. Husband is a pisshead, beat her up, she had to move house, bring three young lads with her. Took a junior position around here. So a quick ride, come on?

'Thanks, Mary.'

'Good luck with your interview.'

The Youthcraft centre is on the outskirts of the county town, near the sand quarry. He walks up the path, seeing sparks from welders dance behind the fogged class of a workshop. A stairs ends in the corner of the entrance hall. Across, there is a door ajar. A small woman with ginger hair stands within, leafing through a red folder. She comes to the office door as the boy looks around.

'Can I help you?' she says.

'I'm here for an interview. My mam called yesterday.'

'Ten o'clock? Oh yes. Please come in.'

The woman sits behind a large pine desk covered with sheets and folders. At the front, next to a large container of pens, there is a black and golden lettered nameplate reading 'Margaret M. Molloy.'

'You can do either mechanics, welding, carpentry, bricklaying or plastering here. You learn some of the basics of the trade and it is envisaged trainees leave in one to two years to take up apprenticeships. The payment for a seventeen-year-old is forty four pounds a week. Is that alright?

'Great,' the boy says.

I start on Monday. I knock on the office door. Margaret M. Molloy opens it.

'Hello. You can go to the welding room for two weeks and see how it goes. It's just over there. Frank will take care of you.' She nods and closes the door.

I knock at the welding room. No one answers. Inside, I hear shouting, hammering, a radio blaring. I open the door. Nobody looks up. A group of blue-overalled boys are working on a huge metal frame.

The teacher, apparently Frank, has grey hair and a white woollen jumper. He sits at a table at the top of the workshop, holding a smouldering chestnut pipe in his hand, scratching stumps of grey stubble on his chin. He looks at me casually.

'Maggie send you in?'

'Yeah.'

'Go over to Malcolm,' Frank points to a stocky youth twisting a long drill bit in his hand.

Along the side of the workshop are small brickwork booths with metal tables, partially hidden behind long black plastic curtains. There is a smell of steel and oil.

'Hello. Started today? Maggie show you the ropes?' Malcolm says.

'Just told me to come in here.'

'You can go in this booth.' Malcolm leads me inside. It's not much bigger than a telephone box. In a vice on the steel table, there is a flat piece of iron. Another piece lies beside it.

'You ever weld before?'

'No,' I says.

'Stick on your earth here, on the table.' Malcom points to something attached below the vice that looks like a jump lead. 'Put your rod in here,' he says, holding up a gun-like implement, connected to a thick black lead. He pushes in a long thin rod and swings the head around. 'You tighten it on. Then hold up your visor like this,' Malcolm continues, taking up a black mask that reminds me of Dart Vader.

'There is one for you.' He nods to another mask hanging in the corner.

Why isn't yer man showing me this? I wonder, looking back to the room. Frank drinks from a mug of tea and then puffs on his pipe.

I can't see anything through the visor.

'This is pure black?' I say, taking it down. There is a blinding flash of light. Malcolm is doing something at the table, sparks fly everywhere. There is a buzzing noise. I hold up the visor and can see just a small green light around the tip of the rod. He is sticking one piece of metal onto the other.

'Now that's tacked,' Malcom says, turning to me. Large purple dots hover in front of me. Malcolm sees me blinking.

'Did you get a flash? Don't look at the light.'

'Why not?'

'You'll know all about it tonight, if you did. Don't worry. It wears off.' Now he tells me. 'Just run the welding rod along the crevice there. That's how you weld,' Malcolm says. It takes me a few attempts to spark off. The rod keeps sticking to the metal and Malcolm has to break each one off, tapping away the stub with a light spring handled hammer.

'At this rate we'll run out of rods,' he says. I am getting cold and bored of this. Eventually, I find I have to scrape the rod on the metal like a match until as it sparks and then gently float it down the crevice. Somehow, it reminds me of fingering a vagina. I get an erection.

The rod shortens as I progress, the heat nears my hand. Malcolm taps away the slag, a brittle shell around the weld run. He examines my weld run.

'Good. Jesus.' Malcolm says. 'That's good for a first time. Very good. Hey Mickey! Mickey!'

A curly-haired boy, smaller and wider than me comes over to our booth. Malcolm points at my work.

'Not bad for a first effort huh?'

218

'Not bad at all,' Mickey says, inspecting the weld. A few others come up.

'What do you think of this?' Mickey says, showing me an oval shaped piece of metal.

'What is it?' I says.

'It's an elephant bullet,' Mickey says.

'Is it yeah?' the boy says.

'Yeah, we have to make them for a crowd in Africa, they ordered them off Frank specially,' Mickey says. 'What do you think of it?'

'Looks fairly dangerous aright,' the boy says.

'Do you know how it works?'

'No. How?'

'You ram it up the elephant's arse and it shoots it out its trunk!' Mickey smacks the boy across the head with the oval shaped metal. He and the others burst out laughing and leave. The boy's head stings, blood drips over his eye.

'I forgot he does that to everyone that's new,' Malcom says. 'Don't make a thing of it. That Mickey is dangerous.'

'Thanks for introducing me,' the boy says.

'Hah-hah,' Malcolm grins. 'You're funny.'

The first night I cannot sleep. My eyes feel like needles are growing out of them. I toss and turn for hours. I wake up late, miss Mary's car and don't get to the centre until half ten.

Frank sends me to Margaret M. Molloy's office.

'You lose a day's pay for being late,' Margaret M. Molloy says simply.

It was because of the flash, but I don't say anything.

Everyone smokes. I buy a packet of ten Major on the way home. I smoke one at the door of the shop. The smoke feels heavy in my lungs.

I tell Melvin about the place at night, while he milks cows, Mann and Conway are still in the school getting down to it, Melvin says, Conway is studying like fuck, I get paid after two weeks, nice twenty pound notes in my pocket, out Friday night, I go for a pint in The Roaring Dog, on the way home sometimes too when I've a few quid left, I get a lift now every morning with Mary in the bank, she wears a skirt most of the time, sometimes I think it gets shorter every week.

A Ford Granada pulls up.

'Hello,' Peter F. Shylock says. The boy gets in. Peter F. Shylock drives fast. The boy is surprised.

'I'm just on the way to the hospital. Mrs Sharpe is very ill, you have heard no doubt?'

'Yeah, bad job.'

'Indeed.'

Doyle said Sharpe was dying of cancer. It is all over her body. Must be all the stress from uniform checks. I think about Doyle. We are kind of friends again now. He met me in the neutrality of Melvin's and we kind of started talking. The incident at the quarry was not mentioned.

'How are you getting on?'

'Not too bad.'

'Where are you these days?'

'I'm in the Youthcraft centre, sir. '

'Very good. Are you there long?

'Nearly a year now, sir.'

'How do you like it?'

'It's aright, it's grand.'

'Good, good. It's great there are such centres available to youths nowadays. In my time, if you didn't study, you had to get the boat to England. But now, there are so many options. A lad could go back and do the leaving a year or two after school, if he wanted. Or even later on as a mature student, that works out very well for some people.' The boy looks out the window at a farmer driving along in a field spreading fertiliser. He looks bored, the boy thinks. 'Have you heard of Doherty Refrigeration?'

'I think so. They run a lot of radio ads?'

'Yes, Peader Doherty. He left school at sixteen. He was a bit wild, to be honest. He was getting into a few scrapes and all the rest of it.'

A few drops of rain land on the windscreen. Peter F. Shylock fiddles with the wiper lever. 'The rubbers are gone in one of those blades, I think. Anyway, he went to do a plumbing course. He got very interested in the engineering side of the work. After about two years, he realised he wanted to get into engineering, refrigeration in particular. But he couldn't do any useful training in the area without a pass Leaving Cert.'

Peter F. Shylock speaks with the same authority he uses on the stage in the assembly hall, yet the volume is a little lower. 'He came to me and asked if he could do the Leaving Cert at the school. We were delighted to offer him as much support as we could. He was a different animal at nineteen, I can tell you. He was up to us every week, looking for excerpts of text books, feedback on things he had written. The teachers were all happy to help him. It was about ten years ago. And do you know what?'

Peter F. Shylock turns to look at the boy, for a second. In the car, he does not move too close, does not invade the personal space. 'He got four As and three Bs. He went on to college and got an honours degree in engineering. He has about twenty vans on the road now, I hear.'

The Granada slows near the Youthcraft centre. Peter Shylock stops the car. 'Look, a lad might want to try out a few things. But the door to education is always open.'

'Fair play to yer man. Thanks for the lift, sir. I hope Mrs Sharpe makes a recovery.'

'We all do, son. Good luck with your course.'

'Thank you, sir.'

The car door closes. Patrick F. Shylock drives away. The boy watches until the car fades from sight. He walks up the path and into the building. Overhead the windows flash from the morning welding class.

Schoolboy is Martin Keaveney's fifth book. It follows the novels *Delia Meade* (2020) and *The Mackon Country* (2021), a novella, *Caravan* (2022) and a short story collection, *The Rainy Day* (2018), all published by Penniless Press. Stage and screen credits include Ireland's national broadcaster RTE and Scripts Ireland Playwriting Festival. He has a PhD in Creative Writing and Textual Studies. Scholarship has been published widely, including at the *New Hibernia Review, Canadian Journal of Irish Studies* and *Estudios Irlandeses*. He was awarded the Sparanacht Ui Eithir for his research in 2016. He works with hundreds of creative writers and literary enthusiasts annually (see more at *www.martinkeaveney.com*).

CARAVAN

Gus Watt has gotten into a bit of a fix. Over the course of 24 hours he meets the woman of his dreams – twice. He is unable to let either down and negotiates the pressures of a relationship with the two Marys with disastrous results. Available worldwide.

'[*Caravan*] offers a rural Ireland full of acute details and nuanced relationships that stay with the reader once the book is finished.'

The Milk House

THE MACKON COUNTRY

Tommy O'Toole is a talented adolescent from a village at the centre of isolated bog swamps knows as the 'Mackon Country'. He lives in a mobile home with his father Joe, who dreams of completing a half-built house in the field. Nights are spent with Uncle Midnight who plays poker while swilling Dutch Gold and recalling hero stories from his time in Lebanon. When Dad gets caught up in a local ATM robbery, Tommy begins a descent into organised crime. Available worldwide.

DELIA MEADE

Now the last of Delia Meade's children have married and moved away, she decides to tidy up the little room under the stairs, known as the Glory-hole. Amongst the forgotten toys, worn-out clothes and dusty boxes of photographs, Delia travels through happy and sad decades of her time at 109, Bog Road. Available worldwide.

'An excellent debut.'

Connaught Telegraph

THE RAINY DAY

Farmers: young and old, cunning, foolish, greedy, generous, talented and forgotten. These and those belonging to them are gathered in this short story collection, sometimes clearly in Ireland's west, but mostly in an unnamed landscape which shapes those often waiting for that rainy day to come. Available worldwide.

'*The Rainy Day* […] will really strike a chord with rural readers.'

Connaught Telegraph